EXTRACURRICULAR MURDER

A Tony Boudreaux Mystery

Other books in the *Tony Boudreaux Mystery* Series:

The Ying on Triad
Death in the Distillery
Skeletons of the Atchafalaya
Galveston
Vicksburg

Other Mysteries by Kent Conwell:

The Riddle of Mystery Inn

Avalon Westerns by Kent Conwell:

Promise to a Dead Man
Bowie's Silver
Angelina Showdown
Gunfight at Frio Canyon
An Eye for an Eye
A Hanging in Hidetown
The Gambling Man
Red River Crossing
A Wagon Train for Brides
Friday's Station
Sidetrip to Sand Springs
The Alamo Trail
Blood Brothers
The Gold of Black Mountain
Glitter of Gold
The Ghost of Blue Bone Mesa
Texas Orphan Train
Painted Comanche Tree
Valley of Gold
Bumpo, Bill, and the Girls
Wild Rose Pass
Cattle Drive to Dodge

EXTRA-CURRICULAR MURDER

A Tony Boudreaux Mystery

•

Kent Conwell

AVALON BOOKS
NEW YORK

All the characters in this book are fictitious,
and any resemblance to actual persons,
living or dead, is purely coincidental.
Published by Thomas Bouregy & Co., Inc.
160 Madison Avenue, New York, NY 10016

Library of Congress Cataloging-in-Publication Data

Conwell, Kent.
Extracurricular murder : a Tony Boudreaux mystery / Kent Conwell.
p. cm.
ISBN 0-8034-9788-1 (acid-free paper)
1. Private investigators—Texas—Austin—Fiction. 2. Murder—Investigation—Fiction. I. Title.

PS3553.O547E9 2006
813'.6—dc22
2006003151

PRINTED IN THE UNITED STATES OF AMERICA
ON ACID-FREE PAPER
BY HADDON CRAFTSMEN, BLOOMSBURG, PENNSYLVANIA

To my son, Todd, who always likes a good mystery.
Try to figure this one out.

And to my wife, Gayle.

Chapter One

"Chance," said Anatole France, "is perhaps the pseudonym God uses when He doesn't want to sign His name." That little gem of wisdom makes a lot more sense to me now than it did last December, primarily because I'd hate to think all of the events that occurred since then had been planned by the God the nuns taught me in my catechisms.

Instead of taking up Danny O'Banion on a free treat out at the County Line Barbecue that night, I should have packed my bags, gathered my gifts, slid my Cajun rear in my pickup, and headed home to Church Point, Louisiana for an early Christmas on the bayou with the alligators and crawfish.

Had I left Austin, I would never have met Frances Holderman. But, I met her, and from that moment on, the tangled machinations of chance began unwinding. Because of the Holderman case, I found myself struggling to pin down the murderer of an ex-stripper's husband; coping with my young cousin who, I discovered too late, fancied himself an up and coming drug lord; and in a final twist of fate, fortune, and fortuity, my on-again, off-again Significant Other, Janice Coffman-Morrison, instead of working at my side in the PI business, dumped me.

* * *

As soon as I saw Frances Holderman, I forgot all about the cold drizzle outside and the hot argument inside between me and my boss, Marty Blevins, who had reneged on a raise.

She was knockdown beautiful—blond, hazel eyes, and pouty lips. She wore a full-length fur coat, faux fur as far as I knew. I couldn't tell alpaca from muskrat. Fur's fur, but I guessed that beneath the coat was probably a sculpted body any twenty-year-old stripper would have envied.

Obviously, Marty felt the same way for he snugged up his tie to his size twenty-two neck and slipped on his wrinkled jacket. He even dumped his overflowing ashtray in the trash, and popped into the lounge to gargle some Listerine hoping to mask his mid-morning shot of bourbon.

But after taking a second, closer look at Holderman, I picked up a trace of hardness beneath that finely chiseled jaw. Her flesh seemed a little too firm, her eyes a little too sharp, her manner a little too direct.

On the other hand, business was business, so I did the polite thing and nodded when Marty introduced me. "Tony Boudreaux here is one of our top investigators," he explained as Frances Holderman extended her hand and gave me a warm smile. Marty must have cringed when he gave me that introduction.

Her hand was tiny and soft, but cold. Her slender fingers squeezed mine, then she withdrew her hand and folded it back in her lap. She arched an eyebrow at Marty, and with a faint, almost challenging smile, replied, "I hope so, Mr. Blevins. I sincerely hope so." She shifted her hazel eyes back to meet mine. "You see, Mr. Boudreaux. If this is not handled properly, I could lose eight million dollars."

Marty gagged.

The office grew silent. Outside, a spray of rain splattered against the window, sounding like a handful of gravel.

I glanced at Marty who had started drooling at the mention of eight million bucks. I didn't blame him. If I hadn't been facing her, I would have drooled too, but I was too busy trying to sound suave and reassuring. I hitched up one leg and plopped down on the edge of Marty's desk. I crossed my arms. "I'm sure you'll be happy with our work, Mrs. Holderman. Blevins Investigations is well known in Austin for client satisfaction."

That was bull, but it sounded good, and Marty ate it up.

From her red purse, she pulled out a silver cigarette case encrusted with diamonds from which she retrieved a Virginia Slim cigarette and held it to her lips between two slender fingers. Her nails were indecently long and, not surprisingly and I wondered if perhaps not symbolically, painted bright red. "Do you mind if I smoke?"

Marty answered her question by falling all over himself to light her cigarette.

After a deep drag, she filled us in on the details in a monotone that suggested she had told and retold the story a thousand times. "My husband, George Holderman, was superintendent of Safford Independent School District south of Austin. He was murdered a year ago. The police are at a dead end, but the case is still open. Consequently, the insurance company, Universal Life, will not pay off on my husband's policy. You see," she said calmly, "I am a suspect because of the amount of the policy and the fact during heated arguments at home and various get-togethers, more than once, and in the presence of others, I threatened to kill George for being unfaithful."

She shrugged noncommittally. "Naturally, the insurance company refuses my claim for the benefits. I want you to find the real murderer. I'm willing to pay up to fifty thousand dollars."

Marty tried not to choke. I could see the dollar signs in his eyes. Finally, he found his voice. "Why, ah, I think we can help, Mrs. Holderman," he replied. "Don't you, Tony?"

I knew what I was supposed to say. "Yeah. We certainly can." But, my brain raced. No PI poked around in a police investigation, especially if he wanted to keep his license. Local police tolerated private investigators like the human race tolerates the common cockroach, like Marty and me had tolerated each other for the last few months.

She eyed me narrowly. The faint smile over her lips remained fixed. "What would you do first, Mr. Boudreaux?"

I shot Marty a glance. His eyes pleaded with me to say the right words. Clearing my throat, I replied, "First, Mrs. Holderman, since your husband's case is still open, I'd make sure the local police have no objection. Second, I'd let the insurance company know we're looking into the matter and that we will share everything we find. As you say, they won't pay off until the real killer is convicted, or until their own investigators are satisfied."

She took another drag and released the smoke slowly, all the while studying me and digesting my reply. "What if the police object, Mr. Boudreaux?"

I nodded to Marty. "That's up to Mr. Blevins. It's his license they could mess with."

Marty cleared his throat. Then, a little too emphatically announced, "That won't be no problem, Mrs. Holderman. I have excellent rapport with local law agencies. I'm quite sure we can come up with a working relationship."

A rumble of thunder rattled the windowpanes, counterpointing his words.

I don't think Marty spotted it, but I saw a hint of skepticism in her eyes. I suddenly had the distinct feeling that dumb blond jokes did not apply to Frances Holderman. "So when can you tell me just what you think you can do, Mr. Blevins?"

Marty's fleshy cheeks colored at her question's hint of his impotence. In his best Humphrey Bogart manner, he growled, "Mrs. Holderman. I guarantee we'll be ready to provide you a contract by this time tomorrow." He paused, then added, "We work on a customary five thousand dollar advance which we bill against. Above that, it's seventy-five dollars an hour and expenses."

Her eyes held his for several seconds. She dropped her gaze

to her purse, retrieved a business card, and handed it to Marty. "Here's my number. I expect to hear from you by noon tomorrow."

Marty took the card with his thick fingers and nodded like a panting bluetick hound. "Don't worry, Mrs. Holderman. We'll do you a good job."

After Frances Holderman left, Marty lost no time in pouring a drink. He loosened his tie and plopped down in the swivel chair behind his battered desk and looked up at me. The splotches of color had faded from his fleshy cheeks. "You know Chief Ramon Pachuca. Check with him and with the insurance company. Find us a starting point on this case."

I narrowed my eyes. "Forget Pachuca. What about my raise?"

He frowned, then shook his head slowly. "Look, Tony. My cash flow is—"

"Bull, Marty. I know better. I'll take this case, but I want my raise just like you promised after I kept Danny O'Banion's nephew from riding the needle in Huntsville."

He stared at me for several long seconds, released a long sigh, then nodded. "Okay. You got it."

I grinned. "All right. Now what about Chief Pachuca?"

"You know him. See if you can get him to give us a hand."

"He's with the Austin force. They got nothing to do with it. Holderman was murdered out in Safford. I don't know anyone out there."

Marty gave me a glazed look. Abruptly, the click of understanding flickered in his eyes. "Yeah. Well, see Pachuca anyway. Maybe he has a contact with the Safford PD."

That was the best we could hope for, I figured. "I'll see what I can do."

Back at my desk, I called Bob Ray Burrus, an old school chum who worked the evidence room for the local police. I wanted some background before I tried my pitch on Chief Pachuca. Quickly, I told him about Holderman's visit. "You got buddies at Safford. You hear anything about it?"

He hesitated. "Not much. There were three or four possibles, but the homicide boys ran into a brick wall at every turn. It's in the open file now."

I grinned. "Open, huh? That probably means it's dead."

"Yeah."

"Thanks, Bob Ray. I owe you, buddy."

Now I was ready to see Chief Pachuca, with whom I'd worked on a couple cases. Despite his dislike for PI's, we'd managed an amiable relationship.

When I stepped into his office, mustachioed Chief Pachuca, a fourth generation Texan, looked up from his desk, his ubiquitous cigar clamped between his teeth. A frown carved deep crevices in his broad forehead. "What are you doing here, Boudreaux? I don't like PIs dripping water on my floor." His cigar bobbed up and down when he spoke.

I grinned sheepishly. There was nothing like being made to feel right at home.

Chapter Two

For the most part, Pachuca was a fair man although his brusque manner suggested he was a world-class jerk. He was as direct and impatient as he was perceptive and meticulous, but in the few instances where we had worked together, we had developed a comfortable, though reserved, relationship.

I brushed the water from the sleeves of my raincoat. "Protocol, Chief. Protocol. And a favor."

He leaned back and studied me with wary eyes. The frown faded from his square face. "For what?"

I gestured to a straight-back chair. "Mind if I sit?"

His eyes narrowed. "You going to be here that long?"

"Depends on you, Chief. You tell me to beat it, I'm gone."

He leaned back in his chair and chuckled. "Sure. Have a seat. Never let it be said Austin's finest don't go out of their way to please the public even though they're making a swimming pool of my office. Now, what are you after?"

I glanced at the water pooling around my feet. "Sorry. But, the reason I'm here is that Frances Holderman paid us a visit today. She wants us to clear her as a suspect in her husband's death."

Pachuca's thin face darkened. His mustache quivered.

"Holderman? You gotta be kidding. The woman is guilty as sin. If it was my jurisdiction, I'd nail her keister to the wall."

I literally backed up a step, his sharp reply taking me by surprise. "Hey, what's going on here? That doesn't sound like you, Ramon."

The veins in his neck bulged. He glared at me for several seconds, and then closed his eyes and leaned back in his chair. "Sorry. It's just that I knew George Holderman. He wasn't no saint, but he was a decent man. Pretty shrewd for the most part except when he married that tramp. Look at her. Almost half his age. He found her in a topless bar over in Elgin doing pole dances." Before I could reply, he continued. "Of course, that was eight, ten years back, but I'll always believe she started planning his murder on their wedding night."

Trying to feel my way through the minefield of his obvious malice toward her, I replied, "I know the Safford department's been working on it, but I heard the investigation has run into a dead end."

He snorted. "You said it. Dead end. I've seen the evidence. Plenty of physical, some circumstantial, but none of it leads anywhere. There were four solid suspects. I don't remember who they are, but your client is one of them."

"Prospective client," I corrected him.

He nodded. "Yeah. Well, I know deep in my gut she's guilty. That witch is staring at an eight million dollar payoff. That's reason enough to kill anybody. Besides, neighbors heard her threaten him." He grimaced and chewed on his cigar. "The way I heard it was there were four or five more teachers plus a couple high school seniors in the area when Holderman got it after a PTA meeting one night."

"High school seniors?"

"Yeah. The principal had two students monitoring the hall with a sign-in sheet."

"Monitoring the hall? At night? During a PTA meeting?

Why? I know they got them during the days, but why at night with just a bunch of adults?"

He shrugged. "Beats me. I told you, it ain't my jurisdiction."

I seized my opportunity. "Look, Chief. She wants us to clear her. You know, my boss is not going to stick his nose where it doesn't belong. The favor I'm asking you is to see if the Safford boys will give us permission to look into the case. We'll turn everything we find over to them. Who knows, maybe we'll stumble across something that might give them the evidence they need."

"Why don't you talk to them?"

I held my hands out to my side. "I don't know anyone out there."

He leaned back in his chair pondering my request, then rocked forward. "For a PI, Boudreaux, you're okay. You've always kept your nose clean and stayed out of our hair. Who knows, you might find something they missed. Maybe you can turn up the evidence to bury that tramp in the hole for the rest of her life."

"Like I said, Chief, all I want is to look into it. Whatever I find, good or bad, goes to Safford PD."

He nodded. "Okay, you still got the insurance company. Maybe they won't like you interfering."

I glanced at the window. The rain had slackened. To the north, a tiny patch of blue eased over the horizon. "Haven't talked to them yet. I figured with you on our side, they won't argue. Besides, they'll see everything we turn up. We're really just helping them out." I kept a straight face.

A frown knit his forehead. He growled. "Who said I'm on your side?"

With a sheepish grin, I replied. "I didn't mean it like that. I meant the insurance company won't say anything if they know you don't have any objections to the investigation."

He eyed me skeptically. "You think that I'll make a difference with them?"

I gave him a crooked grin. "Beats me, Chief, but I have a hunch they'll probably figure that if an irascible old curmudgeon like you has decided to help us, they might as well go along. Besides, I figure the company would like proof one way or another. Hey, you and I both know they're praying she's guilty so they can hold on to that eight million."

With a slow nod, he pursed his lips. "That's motive enough."

I remained silent, but he was right. Eight million was one heck of a motive.

He studied me for a few more seconds, then nodded. "Okay, Boudreaux. I'll play along with you."

"Thanks. By the way, I'd like to see the case files if you can swing it with them. I won't take them from the office."

He nodded, and I rose and headed for the door. "I'll contact the insurance company. When do you think you can arrange for me to see her files?"

He reached for the telephone. "Come back this afternoon around one or so. I'll know something then." He growled, "And Boudreaux."

I stopped at the door and looked back around, puzzled. "Yeah?"

"Don't jack me around."

I held up three fingers. "Scout's honor."

He snorted. "You ain't no scout."

Outside, the rain had stopped, but the dark-bellied clouds suggested more was on the way. A brisk north wind swept across the parking lot. I shivered. Give me sunshine and warm weather, beach bunnies and cold beer. Someone else could have the snowplows and hot toddies.

After leaving the police station, I drove over to Universal Life Insurance Company. The branch manager welcomed the additional probing, not that their opposition would have prevented our investigation. But my *Grandpere* Moise, who farmed with horses as a youngster, always claimed four animals pulling in the same direction plowed a heap more ground than four pulling in opposite directions. The branch manager agreed.

As I headed across the parking lot to my pickup after leaving Universal Life, my cell phone vibrated. I glanced at the number. Janice Coffman-Morrison, my on-again, off-again Significant Other, one of Austin's poor little rich girls. A smile leaped to my lips when I remembered tonight was the night I had promised her some blackened redfish, and she had promised me dessert.

My smile broadened. Today had been a good day. A raise, a new case, willing cooperation from the local police, full collaboration from the insurance company, and a wonderful evening with Janice. What more could I ask?

I turned the phone on. "Hey. How are you doing? Ready for tonight? I have a new case you might like to hear about."

She ignored my question. Her voice was cool and restrained. "Tony, I'm breaking up with you."

Chapter Three

A sudden gust of wind whipped the lapel of my raincoat against my face, stinging my cheek. I stammered, refusing to believe my ears. "Janice? I couldn't understand you. The wind's blowing hard here."

Very matter-of-factly, she answered, "You heard me, Tony. Our relationship has run its course. You're a sweet boy, but over the years, you've remained the same. I've grown. I'm not cut out for your kind of business or life. I'm a bigger person now, and I'm ready to move on with my life."

"But—"

In the same cool, imperious voice she used when she commanded sommeliers, maitre d's, and waiters, she continued. "No. It's better this way. I don't want to hurt you, but I've got to be honest. This is for the best. Believe me."

"But—"

"No. Trust me, Tony. I know you'll hurt, but the hurt will pass, and you'll see I'm right."

"But—"

"Good-bye, Tony."

Obviously, my less than eloquent rebuttals were having no

effect on her. Before I could stammer, stutter, or spit, she hung up. Immediately, I dialed her number. No answer.

"Come on, Janice. I know you're there. Pick up the phone." On the twentieth ring, I hung up.

I glanced at my watch. Almost one o'clock. Time to get back to the police station. I didn't want Chief Pachuca to change his mind about cooperating with us. Afterward, I'd drop by Janice's and see what set her off this time.

Her aunt had more money than the Bank of England, and Janice, being the only heir, had whatever she desired, whether it be clothes, sports car, or male companionship. That silver spoon of hers permitted her to change her mind on a whim, which she did quite often.

We had met a few years back when I was helping her out of an insurance jam. Neither she nor I were interested in getting serious, but we had fun together even though I quickly realized I was simply a dependable escort, an occasional lover (at her whim), and a frequent confidant.

While the truth of our relationship did batter at my ego in the beginning, I came to terms with the fact that I was simply a tool to satisfy her needs. But, the fact she served the same purpose for me made the entire relationship palpable. We were both fairly content—products of a liberated society.

Inexplicably, despite the skewed relationship between us, we became very good friends who enjoyed each other's company. Personally, I'd never been able to figure out 'our relationship,' as Janice referred to it, but then, I really never worried about it. I seldom paid serious attention to those psychological or personal relationship things. That was a woman's domain. Give me a compelling soccer match between Oman and Turkmenistan anytime.

Ignoring my own skepticism, I had truly figured that our relationship had advanced to the next level when she insisted on working with me on my previous case when we saved an innocent man from execution by the state of Texas.

But now, I felt a nagging ache in the pit of my stomach. I'd often thought that when Janice and I parted ways, I'd shrug and find another partner at the next singles' bar. Now, I wasn't too sure.

During the drive back to the police station, a hundred different reasons for her sudden announcement raced through my head. When I pulled into the parking lot, I still didn't have the foggiest explanation for her decision. The answer, I later learned, was the one reason that never entered my egotistical male mind.

Chief Ramon Pachuca was better than his word. He met me at the door. "What kind of word processing program you use?"

Surprised, I replied with my most articulate "Huh?"

He held up a disk and a manila envelope. "Here's the file. Everything. Pictures, sketches in the envelope. Interview's on the disk. Word Perfect. Billy Vanbiber is the chief at Safford. A good friend. Won't hurt to stop by and meet him. Thank him personally. You hear?"

I made no reference to the almost antiquated Word Perfect and disk. Seemed like the agencies relying on tax money to operate were always two or three generations behind in technology. I simply nodded. "Yeah. I will." I took the evidence. "I use Microsoft Word, but it'll convert to his program."

"Good luck." He turned back into the building, then hesitated. "By the way, I contacted Howard Birnam. He's the principal at Safford High where the body was found. Give him a call. He's expecting you."

I was flattered at Chief Pachuca's consideration in obtaining me the disk, but his paving the way for me with the high school principal left me speechless. I nodded and choked out "Thanks."

He studied me a moment. "Like I told you, Boudreaux. It's nothing benevolent on my part. I just hope you find proof enough to burn that witch."

* * *

A slow drizzle began to fall. On the way home, I swung by Janice's condo, but her Miata was gone, and when the Miata was gone, Janice was gone. I headed home, stopping at a nearby HEB supermarket for a frozen pizza. On impulse, I reached for a six-pack of Old Milwaukee beer. I hesitated, remembering my AA oaths. Then I thought of Janice and picked up a six-pack anyway.

I hesitated in the meat section of the supermarket, eyeing the redfish laid out in display on a bed of ice in the meat case. My thoughts went back to Janice. I muttered a soft curse. Tonight, I should have been buying redfish and chardonnay for an intimate dinner for two, not beer and pizza just for me.

Outside, the drizzle turned into a downpour.

I pulled into my drive and parked under the carport. I made a mad dash through the rain for the porch. Just as I turned the key in the lock, I heard a pitiful meow. I glanced at the base of the neatly trimmed hedge of wax leaf ligustrum and spotted a bedraggled kitten, its long gray hair plastered to his thin body.

As soon as I opened the door, the kitten shot inside and promptly scooted under the couch. I muttered a curse. "All right," I muttered, kicking the door shut and carrying the pizza and beer to the kitchen. "But don't plan on staying around," I called over my shoulder.

As I stood in front of the refrigerator, something brushed my ankle. I glanced down and the kitten was looking up at me. "You hungry? Probably so," I said gruffly. "Okay, I'll give you some milk, but that's it. Understand?"

I sniffed the milk to see if it was still good, then poured some in a bowl, nuked it, and slid it in front of him, after which I popped open a beer and called Marty, apprising him of the fact we had police cooperation. "So now, you can give Holderman a call," I said.

He thanked me profusely, then hung up. I plopped in front of my computer, which over the last few years had come to mean more to me than my Silverado pickup.

When Marty first hired me, I did skips and warrants. His Skip Tracing process was a hit or miss procedure so I set up a procedure utilizing a list of four identifiers that separated one individual from all others with the same name.

By blind luck, I discovered my computer could access hundreds of databases on the Internet. Consequently, I doubled Marty's skip business, earning his gratitude and a raise.

I opened the file on George Holderman, 58, Caucasian, found dead in Room 247, Perry Jacobs' American History classroom at Safford High School. Weapons—a thirty-six-inch Black Barrel baseball bat and an eight and threequarter-inch switchblade.

Pulling out a new pack of 3 × 5 cards, I began taking notes although I had all the information in my computer. Individual cards permitted me to shift information from one context to another, sometimes triggering dramatic and unexpected conclusions. And sometimes not.

I spent the remainder of the afternoon studying the report and taking notes. I was curious as to the principal's rationale for a sign-in list for teachers at a PTA meeting. Of course, school administrators did strange things. I knew that from the experience of having taught English in a high school that preferred king football over academics.

Shivers ran up my spine when I read the ME's autopsy report. In the Medical Examiner's opinion, one of the purported murder weapons, a thirty-six-inch Black Barrel baseball bat, had delivered a crushing blow to the right side of Holderman's forehead, which rendered the victim unconscious. The exsanguinating trauma of the blow and the second weapon, a switchblade knife, having penetrated the subject's heart, precipitated an internal bleed out.

Leaning forward, I studied a photo of the knife protruding from Holderman's chest. It was a blue switchblade with a stainless steel blade and bolster-lock release. Available everywhere, the knife was the kind anyone, even an individual unfamiliar with it, could easily open. Just press the magic button.

Why both a ball bat and a knife? I frowned, but then maybe I was looking too deep. Maybe the killer, after knocking Holderman out, simply wanted to make sure the superintendent was dead.

Thumbing through the file, I discovered the investigating officers had the same question on the use of two weapons, and believe it or not, drew the same conclusion, that the perpetrator wanted to make sure Holderman's ticket was good and punched for the Highway to Heaven or the Staircase to Hades, whichever might be his destination.

Another photo showed the baseball bat on the floor.

That the right side of his forehead was crushed indicated the blow was delivered from the left, signifying perhaps a left-handed perpetrator.

I continued reading the report. There were no bruises on Holderman's forearms, suggesting no chance to fight off his attacker. It appeared that Holderman had been surprised. He stood facing the desk, heard a noise behind him, and turned just as the killer swung. Caught off guard, Holderman had no time to throw up his arms in defense.

I skimmed the list of suspects the detectives interviewed, seven of them, and then read the official reports. After poring over the enormous amount of notes, I gleaned four suspects, the same four the Safford Police Department came up with; Frances Holderman, maiden name Laurent, ex-stripper and betrayed wife; Kim Nally, ex-mistress; Fred Seebell, cuckolded husband of Eunice Seebell, Holderman's one-time secretary; and Perry Jacobs, a history teacher frightened of losing his job.

When I finished reading the file, I leaned back and stared at the computer screen. The Safford PD had put in a lot of work. There were three hundred and eighty pages of thoroughly gathered evidence. Like Chief Pachuca said, plenty of physical evidence, some corpus delicti evidence, some associative evidence, but none that would firmly connect any of the suspects to the crime.

I studied the data, reminding myself of one unequivocal, indisputable, incontestable fact. Evidence does not lie. It cannot be intimidated. It does not forget. It doesn't get excited. It simply sits and waits to be detected, preserved, evaluated, and explained.

Witnesses may lie, lawyers may lie, judges may lie, but not evidence. And since it doesn't, then either not enough had been gathered or that which had been gathered had been interpreted incorrectly.

That was my job, to gather more evidence and do my best to interpret it correctly. I just hoped I was good enough to carry out the job.

Chapter Four

The remainder of the evening I spent studying the files and calling Janice. No answer. Around 10, I gave up and salved my wounded ego with the reminder that neither she nor I had made any personal commitments. This wasn't the first time she'd broken up with me, and if the past was indeed prologue, it wouldn't be the last.

I briefly laid out my plans for the next day, beginning with Howard Birnam, the Safford High School principal after which I would interview his teachers. Later on in the day, I'd visit Frances Holderman and Fred Seebell.

I saw now the strangulated dead end in which the Safford police had found themselves. Not one of the suspects was left-handed, and all had airtight alibis.

I wandered over to the front window. Holding the curtain back with the tip of my finger, I stared into the night, watching the passing cars on the shiny street without seeing them.

Often evidence can be viewed from various angles. And these various perspectives can raise new and intriguing questions. Other times, evidence is absolute in its perspective, as absolute as none of the suspects being left-handed.

The abrupt jangling of the telephone broke into my thoughts. It was my cousin, Leroi Thibodeaux, from Opelousas, Louisiana, the son of my Uncle Patric and his deceased wife, Lantana, a Louisiana Redbone from Beauregard Parish along the Sabine River.

We exchanged pleasantries, but from his tone, I sensed trouble. I was right. “I need some help, Tony. Stewart is on the way to Austin.”

“Stewart? Your Stewart?”

“Yeah. The boy, he left this morning. We tried to talk him out of it, but he claims he’s got connections over there for a good job.”

His tone suggested something more than a father’s reluctance to see his son leave home. “How old is Stewart now, twenty or so?”

“Twenty-two.”

“Hey, Leroi. He’s a man now. If I remember right, you were out on your own at seventeen.”

He grunted. “That was then. This is now.”

I knew exactly what he meant. “Hey, bro, don’t sweat it. He’ll be fine. You did tell him he could stay at my place until he gets settled?”

“Yeah. Hope you don’t mind.” He paused, then added, “Me and Sally will feel better knowing he’s staying with you, at least until the boy, he gets on his feet. Kick his tail if you gots to.”

“Glad to, and don’t worry, he’ll be okay.”

“I sure hope so.” His tentative reply suggested that he had more on his mind. He cleared his throat. “I gots to be honest with you, Tony. Truth is, Sally and me, we’s worried about the boy. We think he might be into drugs.”

The announcement stunned me. “Stewart? Come on, Leroi. Are you sure?”

He hesitated. “Well, not exactly. Sally, she found a couple joints in his car—you know how snoopy mothers can be. Well, anyway, he claimed they weren't his. One of his friends left them." He drew a deep breath. "We had a big argument. Two days later, he gots this job in Austin. Sally and me is worried sick." After a long sigh, he added, "Now, if you don't want him around, we'll understand."

I closed my eyes and muttered a curse. Drugs. Stupid kids. Stupid, dumb kids. I kept my tone light. "Don't say that, Leroi. We're family. Of course, I want Stewart around. I'll see what I can find out for you. You're probably mistaken, you know. You were always kind of slow," I replied, my words light with sarcasm.

Leroi laughed. "You know where you can go."

"Hey, cuz. I'm already there." I paused a moment, then grew serious again. "I'll call when he gets in. Don't worry. Everything will be okay."

After replacing the receiver, I leaned back in my chair and stared at it, turning the last few minutes over in my head. I hoped all that had happened was nothing more than a young man trying to assert his own independence from his father.

I knew from experience that Leroi could be demanding. More than once when we were growing up, we tangled because he was so hard-headed—actually, because we were both so hard-headed.

"I hope that's all there is to it," I muttered, closing my eyes and saying a short little prayer that if my little cousin needed help, I would be capable of providing it.

Later, I searched the apartment for the gray kitten, determined to put him, or her, back outside, but the little sneak had vanished.

When I came out of the bathroom, I jerked to a halt. There he was, curled up on the pillow next to mine, sound asleep, purring like a tiny motorboat.

All I could do was shake my head. "All right. Just for tonight.

Tomorrow, you go," I grumbled, taking care to spread a couple of newspapers on the floor.

The insistent chiming of the doorbell awakened me just after one. Figuring it was Stewart, I pulled on my robe and hurried to the door.

I was right.

Swaying on his feet, Stewart stood in the drizzle, his eyes glazed and a silly grin on his face. "Hey, bro. I made it." He slurred his words.

I glanced over his shoulder. He had parked his Pontiac at the curb. "Get in here out of the rain, Stewart." I reached out and pulled him inside. "Hurry up."

Even though I'd downed a couple of beers a few hours earlier, I still could smell the sweet-sour stench of whiskey on his breath. He staggered inside and promptly passed out on the couch. I threw a couple of blankets over him and called Leroi to put his mind to rest, but without mentioning his son's inebriation.

When I turned back to the bedroom, guess who was standing in the doorway, watching the excitement? The kitten, his ears perked forward, his tail straight up in the air, curled on the tip like a question mark. When I started toward him, he spun and raced back to the bed.

During the night, the rain ceased. I rose early to a cloudless and chilled sky. At seven, I dialed Safford High School. Birnam was very agreeable. We made a nine o'clock appointment. Safford was south, halfway between Austin and Bastrop, around twenty or twenty-five miles from my apartment, an hour-long drive thanks to Austin traffic.

Quickly, I showered, shaved, and slipped into my usual attire of washed out jeans, sport shirt, tweed jacket, and boots. I jammed a bagel in my jacket and filled an insulated cup with coffee. I was ready to take on the day.

I checked on Stewart who still slept. I left him a note, a bottle of aspirin, and my cell phone number with instructions to give me a call.

I wanted to talk to him, try to find out just what was going on.

Chapter Five

Principal Howard Birnam was swamped with problems, several of which I spotted as his secretary led me down a hall lined on either side with surly students standing shoulder-to-shoulder waiting to see either Birnam or one of the assistant principals.

The girls must have taken their fashion tips from the good-time girls who strutted up and down Sixth Street, nose rings and all. The boys, well, the kindest thing to say about them was they probably couldn't even spell fashion.

We halted at a closed door. His secretary tapped, cracked it open, stuck her head inside, and then pushed the door wide. "Please come in, Mr. Boudreaux."

Howard Birnam came around the desk with a warm smile on his face. He extended his hand. "Glad to meet you, Mr. Boudreaux. Personally, I'm extremely pleased you're here. Maybe you can solve this mess." He indicated a chair across the desk from him. He continued, explaining how the unsolved murder had created unnecessary tension among the faculty, how the students were experiencing difficulty in putting it behind them, and how in general, the incident had disrupted the routine at Safford High School.

"I'm going to give it my best shot, Mr. Birnam."

He grinned and leaned back. "The name's Howard. And I'm at your disposal at any time, day or night."

"Mine's Tony."

He slid a sheet of paper across the desk. "Here's a roster of our teachers. If you want, we can set up appointments throughout the day. We'll handle it however you want."

I pulled a slip from my jacket and handed it to Birnam. "These are the ones I need to see first."

He read off their names. "Kim Nally, Perry Jacobs, Dorothy Saussy, Harper Weems, Jim Hawkins, Henry Bishop, Lionel Portis and the hall monitors." When he finished, he looked at me with a quizzical expression on his face.

I chuckled. "Those were the names on the police report, Howard. I'd like to see them today, if I can."

"No problem." He picked up the telephone and punched a number. "Mrs. Thomas. Please line up meetings with the following teachers during their conference period with Mr. Boudreaux in the ARD room."

He read off the list, nodded as she repeated his instruction, then replaced the receiver and pushed back from his desk. "Now, let me show you to the ARD room."

I stopped him. "Before we go, tell me about Holderman. Did you know him very well?"

Half raised from his chair, he hesitated, then plopped back down. "Only at school. He was an ambitious man. I was surprised he stayed as long as he did. From time to time, he polarized the school board, but he always got his contract extended."

I jotted the information on my note cards. "Any enemies?"

The square-jawed principal shook his head. "He was tough, but he was fair. Oh, he might have had some personality conflicts with various teachers, but I got along with him fine. I've been at a loss as to why he was murdered."

Nodding to the list I had given him, I asked, "You hear any talk about those names?"

"Yeah." He arched an eyebrow. "Just talk though. Nothing substantive as far as I'm concerned."

"Oh?"

He leaned forward. "Let me put it this way, Tony. Every teacher on that list does me an excellent job. None have given me any reason to believe any of the rumors. Now, some of the gossip might be true, but if it is, I don't know of it."

I studied him for a few seconds. His level gaze, his faint smile reinforced my belief that he was telling me the truth as he saw it. "One more question."

"Shoot."

"Why hall monitors? And a sign-in sheet for PTA meetings at night? I taught English at Madison High over in Austin. We never had any sign-in sheets. We just showed up when we were supposed to."

He gave me a wry grin. "That's how it used to be here until George Holderman arrived. George wanted to know everything that went on in the district. He and I agreed on the monitors to control the kids running the halls while their parents were at various meetings in the building. The other, the sign-in sheets, we disagreed. My teachers are professionals. A sign-in is a slap in the face." He gave a sheepish shrug. "I thought it foolish, but he was my boss. If that's what he wanted, that's what I did."

"You said sheets? More than one sign-in sheet?"

Arching an eyebrow, he grinned sheepishly. "We sign in for every meeting, and if a teacher wants to go to his classroom after hours, he has to sign in also."

I whistled softly, relieved I had left the business when I did. "What about now?"

The principal grinned. "Guess."

I chuckled. "Smart man." I rose and extended my hand. "Thanks, Howard."

"You're welcome." He hesitated. "You said you taught English at Madison?"

I nodded. "Years ago."

"Why'd you get out of the business?"

With a crooked grin, I replied, "Politics and parents."

He chuckled. "I know the feeling. Come on. I'll show you the ARD room."

Following him from his office, I sensed he was probably one of the few dedicated educators in the system today. I envied the kids in his school, nose rings and all.

The ARD room was a small cubicle where the counselors, parents, and diagnosticians for the special needs students regularly met to monitor students' progress. The only furniture in the room was a round table and six chairs, a nice, cozy arrangement where everyone had to face everyone and no one could duck a question.

He introduced me to the counselors, the secretary, and the registrar, after which he pointed out the unisex bathroom and the nook housing the coffee. "Help yourself. Usually, it's fresh."

The phone rang. Birnam answered, cut his eyes to me, and nodded. "Thank you, Mrs. Thomas."

He replaced the receiver. "We have a few minutes before Kim Nally gets here. Care for some coffee?"

"Sure."

The coffee was fresh, steaming, and Cajun strong. Gingerly I sipped at it. "Now, this is what I call good coffee."

Birnam blew across the surface. "This is my singular journey into the Cajun culture, Mr. Boudreaux." He nodded to the smiling secretary. "Rita Viator is our resident Cajun, straight from Lafayette. She's bound and determined to create a sense of appreciation in our taste buds for Cajun cuisine."

She shot us a mischievous smile. "Oh mon no, Mr. Birnam. The coffee, she is supposed to be strong." Rita Viator appeared to be in her fifties, reminding me of my good-natured *grand-mere* who laughed constantly and related anecdotes with the best of the yarn spinners.

He laughed. "Well, you succeeded again, Rita."

I inhaled the rich fragrance of the coffee and grinned at her. "Delicious. Like back home. I'm from Church Point, northwest of Lafayette." At the mention of Church Point, I couldn't help thinking about Stewart and wondering how his hangover was treating him. I needed to call him at the first opportunity.

"Oh mon no. My family, the old ones, they be from Lawtell."

For the next few minutes, we exchanged stories and recollections of back home, from the swamps of Atchafalaya to the boudain of Eunice, to the cockfights of Cankton. It had been several months since I had heard the lilting patois of Cajun country. Made me homesick.

I glanced around as the glass doors of the counselors' office opened and a slender, dark-complexioned woman in blue sweats with Safford High School emblazoned across the front entered. She paused, surveyed the room, focused on Birnam, and strode toward us. She gave me a wary glance, then directed her words to Birnam. "You wanted to see me, Howard?"

"Yeah, Kim. This is Tony Boudreaux. He's here looking into the George Holderman thing."

She rolled her eyes as if to say, not again.

Chapter Six

Sensing her impatience, I spoke up. "Look, Mrs. Nally. I'm just a private investigator working for Mrs. Holderman who retained us to clear the case. The Safford police have given us permission to talk to everyone. I don't want to impose or dredge up bad memories, so I promise I'll be as brief as I can." I gave her my best little boy, come hither smile.

She studied me a moment, then shook her head and gave Birnam a frustrated look. "Might as well, Howard. They're going to keep coming back until the thing is beat to death."

"Great." I offered my hand. "The name's Tony."

She gave me a bright smile that contrasted attractively with her tanned skin. "Mine's Kim."

Birnam gave a brief nod. "You can use the ARD room."

I poured another cup of Rita's coffee and offered some to Kim. She declined with a knowing grin. "Rita's brew is a little too strong for me." She winked at the grinning secretary and added with a mischievous curl on her lips, "But sometimes I do use it for liniment for my girls' sore muscles."

I studied her as she walked ahead of me, remembering the police report. Kim Nally, 34-year-old PE teacher who had an affair with the superintendent, and whose personalized pen

Holderman had given her was found beside the dead man on Perry Jacobs' desk. Her alibi was Dorothy Saussy, an algebra teacher, who had been visiting in Nally's office around the time of the murder.

We sat at the table, and I pulled out my notebook, opened it to a blank page, and handed it to her. "If you don't mind, I'd like your name and telephone in case I have to get in touch with you again concerning the case."

For a moment, she hesitated, an eyebrow arched. With a shrug, she put down the information and slid the notepad and pen back to me, all with her right hand.

That answered one of my questions. "I read the reports. If you don't mind, just tell me what you told the police."

"Why not?" She leaned forward, resting her elbows on the table. Her eyes fixed on mine. "The reason the police talked to me was that George and I had an affair, one I broke off two years ago." She stressed *I*. "You see, I'm a single mother with a seven-year-old autistic daughter. I might not be a rocket scientist, Mr. Boudreaux, but I am smart enough to realize that messing around with the superintendent of the school district was a shortcut to disaster." She lifted both eyebrows in a gesture of resignation. "So, I broke it off."

I glanced at my notes. "You stated that you were in your room from about eight-forty-five P.M. until the body was discovered."

"Yes." She leaned back, keeping her eyes fixed on mine. There was a gleam of defiance in her dark eyes, as if she was daring me to accuse her of the murder. "I was visiting with Dorothy Saussy. She teaches algebra. She's a single mother also, and we were discussing sitters. She left around nine-thirty when Linda May and Iona Flores stopped by to pick her up. The three of them then went to Dorothy's room to work on curriculum."

I jotted the last two names in my notebook. "I don't remember seeing their names on the police report."

With a shrug, she replied. "That's the cops' problem. I told the officer."

"What were you doing in your room so late anyway?"

She uttered a soft groan. "PTA. The superintendent insisted all teachers attend all PTA meetings. He even demanded we sign in and out at the table outside the auditorium."

"In and out?"

"Yes. Something, huh?"

"Must have been an unpleasant joker to work for."

"Yes and no." She glanced at the table, then lifted her eyes, still defiant. "He wasn't a bad man. He just wanted what he wanted too badly. He tried to run over people, and obviously, someone stopped him."

"Obviously."

She chuckled. "It was strictly physical between me and George. He was powerful. I liked that. I think I was probably somewhat infatuated at first, but after a while, real life sort of elbowed infatuation aside, and I realized he was nowhere near the icon I first thought. But the truth of the matter was I enjoyed being with him." Her gaze swept over me, and a wicked smile curled her lips. "Nothing special, but he was okay."

I felt my ears burn. The naughty little grin playing across her Sunday School teacher's lips broadened, as if enjoying my discomfort. "George tried to do more than he was capable."

Momentarily confused, I couldn't decide if she were talking about his prowess or his business ambitions. "According to my notes," I mumbled, flipping through the pages and changing the subject, "there was a reception after the meeting. Were you there?"

She shrugged. "No. I went up to my room to get some work taken care of. I hate wasting time standing around and visiting with others. Then Dorothy showed up."

"And she left at nine-thirty."

"A little after, with the other teachers."

"The Medical Examiner figures Holderman died somewhere between nine and nine-thirty. I think that's when a teacher named Perry Jacobs found him."

"Yeah." She dropped her gaze. "I was working on basketball plays when I heard Perry shout. I ran out into the hall. He was standing in his doorway a couple rooms down, staring into his room."

"Then what?"

"When he saw me, he ran for the stairs."

Whoa. Someone running down the stairs? Here was a small item that had not been covered in the initial interrogation. I played dumb, which really wasn't all that difficult. "I don't think I remember seeing anything about that in the police report."

"Probably not. Perry figured it was just his imagination. I don't guess he saw any sense in mentioning it."

"Then what?"

"Then I ran into Perry's room and saw George draped over the desk."

"Over the desk?"

Her tanned face crumpled into a grimace. "Yeah. On his back. And"—she hesitated, closed her eyes, swallowed hard, and blurted out—"a knife in his chest."

"What about Perry Jacobs?"

"I ran after him, and met him coming back up the stairs."

"Where had he gone?"

She raised an eyebrow. "He said he thought he saw someone run around the corner and down the stairs. When he got down there, all he found was Harper Weems. Harp hadn't seen anyone."

"Who is Harper Weems?"

"Harp? He teaches English and is the school photographer. Nice guy. Physically challenged. He has to use a wheelchair. He's paralyzed from the waist down. But he's always trying to help the kids. Very conscientious teacher."

I arched an eyebrow.

She continued. "Not just with school business, but with their other problems also." She shook her head. "He's a good man. And a good man is hard to find nowadays. I asked him once why he didn't request a room in the new wing designed for the handicapped, but he'd been in that old room ever since he began teaching and didn't want to leave." She arched an eyebrow skeptically. "He claimed he liked the ambiance of the older wing. Said it helped bring literature to life. He's sort of romantic that way. You know, like a lot of English teachers."

As an ex-English teacher, I shifted uncomfortably in my chair. "He'd been to PTA also, huh?"

"I told you, everyone had to go. The cops just talked to him because he was in his room downstairs. I suppose they talked to anyone who was around."

I jotted a few notations, then scanned my notes. "Just a couple of more questions, Kim. Your pen, the one Holderman gave you. How did it end up in Jacobs' room?"

"Beats me. Probably Perry needed a pen and grabbed one off my desk. I keep a pen and pencil box on my desk in case a student needs one during class. A couple of times, Perry borrowed some. He might have borrowed that one."

She made sense. I remembered my teaching days. Pretty much the way she said it. Pencils on the desk for forgetful kids. I closed my notebook. "I appreciate your time, Kim. I guess that's about it." I hesitated, then out of curiosity, commented, "I taught over at Madison High in Austin a few years back. All of the coaches had their offices on the first floor of the gym where they could keep their eyes on the boys. How come yours is on the second?"

"You taught, huh? What'd you teach?"

I grinned. "English."

Her eyes danced. "So you're one of those romantics too, huh? Like Harp?"

"Not really. I guess if I were, I'd still be in the business. But tell me, why is your office on the second floor?"

A wry grin twisted her lips. "You said it earlier, Tony. Eyes on the boys. Yeah, the men coaches get on the first floor, and the ladies have to convert a storeroom on the second for their office. The way of the world, the school world that is." Despite her exaggerated indifference, I sensed a trace of bitterness in her words.

"I can't argue that. I guess we're all just a bunch of male chauvinist pigs."

She pushed back from the table. "I couldn't have said it any better." She offered her hand. "I hope I've been helpful."

I followed her out of the small room and headed for some more of Rita's coffee. The secretary glanced up as I approached. I indicated the coffee. "Tastes like Seaport," I said, naming the favorite coffee back in Church Point.

Rita beamed at the compliment. "I buy it by the case." While I poured another cup, she glanced after Kim Nally who disappeared out the door. "She a nice girl."

I glanced at Rita, sensing there was something she wanted to say. "Have you known her long?"

"Long enough. The girl, she a good person. Sometimes, her head is on crooked, but she a good mother, a good teacher." In a very casual, conversational tone, she asked, "She tell you about the abortion?"

I tried not to choke on my coffee. "Abortion?"

Rita looked up at me with the same sort of pained tolerance on her face that a mother wears when her child has deliberately skirted the truth. "No. Me, I think she wouldn't. Holderman, he was no good. She get pregnant. Mrs. Holderman, that woman swear a big scandal, so there is abortion. All is kept hush-hush, but it do happen."

Finishing my coffee, I tossed the cup in the trash and winked at Rita. "Thanks. Us Cajuns got to stick together."

Her eyes danced. "I say so."

* * *

Perry Jacobs was next. The number one suspect as far as I was concerned despite his alibi. For two reasons; first Holderman had been murdered in Jacobs' room, and second, Jacobs' contract was not to be renewed at the end of the year.

I glanced at my watch. I had another thirty minutes before the history teacher was to arrive. Stepping next to a window, I pulled out my cell and called Stewart. I grimaced. No answer. Maybe he was still asleep. I left a message on my phone on the outside chance he might pick it up.

I turned to Rita. "How about pointing me in the direction of Perry Jacobs' room. I'd kinda like to wander the halls for a few minutes."

Besides, I needed to consider the new information about the abortion. If Holderman had forced her to abort, Nally had herself a dandy motive. Revenge. Anyone who faced the rigors of raising an autistic child did not seem like one who would easily accommodate abortion. If she was forced, the anger she harbored could be mighty powerful. No, Kim Nally was not beyond suspect.

Chapter Seven

Room 247 was at the northwest end of the school, which was laid out like a U. The wing in which Holderman was murdered contained sixty-four rooms, thirty-two on each floor, sixteen on each side of the hall. Three stairways, one at each end of the wing and one in the middle, served the second floor. The hall monitors had been set up at the entrance to the wing the night of the murder.

From the information Kim Nally gave me, I found the women coaches' office just as she had said, a couple of doors down from Jacobs' room, which was three doors from the stairway at the end of the hall. Five rooms in the opposite direction was the middle flight of stairs.

Peering into the empty room, I saw that it was a typical classroom, a blackboard on the front wall, a teacher's desk, thirty-odd student chairs, shelves and a coat closet along the back wall. I tried to visualize George Holderman facing the desk with the killer creeping stealthily from the rear, bat poised. I glanced again at the closet.

Two theories popped into my head. Either the killer was someone the superintendent knew or the killer had hidden in the closet. Glancing up and down the empty hall, I slipped into the room and opened the closet door. A jacket, few books, umbrella, and a tube of rolled-up maps, leaving room for someone to hide.

Back out in the hall, I took the end stairway, at the base of which was an open classroom door. I glanced inside and spotted a man in a wheelchair at the front of the room. Harper Weems. One wall of his room was covered with framed photographs, landscape, sports, portraits, an eclectic collection. Bookcases sat on either side of the blackboard behind the teacher's desk. A camera was on the corner of his desk.

I looked up and down the hall. My morning coffee was catching up with me. A couple of doors down was the boys' restroom, a typical, forty-year-old facility. Urinals lined one wall, and commodes separated by tiled walls lined the other. Despite its age, it was spotlessly clean and fragrant.

The bell rang while I was washing my hands. I dried on the paper towels, then sauntered into the hallway, watching the tide of laughing, shouting students sweep past.

Harper Weems rolled into the hall, expertly backing his chair next to the wall so he could monitor the hallway, a duty I had enjoyed for it always provided informal bantering with the students. He ran his fingers through his long blond hair.

Most of the passing students chattered or waved to him, gestures he returned with a warm smile and a wave. A slender man around forty, he appeared to have a strong upper body, with little of the physical deterioration sometimes evident in the physically challenged.

I eased along the wall to him. "Mr. Weems?" I had to talk over the hubbub of the students.

He smiled up at me. "One and the same."

"Tony Boudreaux." I extended my hand.

"Ah, Mr. Boudreaux. Nice to meet you. Unless I read it wrong, I got a note last period to meet with you down in the counselors' office near the end of this period." His grip was firm. And like most teachers, his hand was smooth and soft. I noticed he wasn't wearing a watch.

"I was just wandering the building before I met with Perry Jacobs." I nodded to the students streaming past. "Well behaved."

He laughed. "They're good kids. Mischievous, but basically good, intelligent youngsters. It's a thrill to work with them."

His room was empty. I nodded inside. "Look, if you want, we can take care of business now. Jacobs isn't due for another fifteen minutes."

His smile faded. "Just what business are you talking about, Mr. Boudreaux?"

I handed him a card and brought him quickly up to date on Frances Holderman's request. "All I'm doing is going over what you told the police."

He arched an eyebrow and shrugged. "Sure. Where do I start?"

I cleared my throat. "At the beginning. PTA."

He had to lean forward to hear above the noise of the passing students. He indicated to his room. "Let's go inside. We can hear better." He rolled ahead of me. The right wheel of his chair squeaked.

He closed the door, leaving the noise out in the hall. By contrast, his room was as silent as a sepulcher. He motioned me to a student desk, but I declined. With a shrug, he began. "I don't know much of anything about what happened. Like I told the police, after the PTA meeting, I came down here to do some grading. I went into the boys' restroom, and when I came out, Perry was running down the stairs. He asked if I'd seen anyone in the hall. I hadn't. And that was it."

I frowned. "He just went back upstairs then?"

"Yes."

"Did you go up there?" I glanced at his legs. My ears burned. "I mean, elevator or something."

He shook his head. "No. This is an old wing. No elevators. That's why they keep me on the first floor."

I sensed a touch of wry sarcasm in his last remark. "That night, did Perry Jacobs tell you what happened?"

"Yeah. Well, he told me about the superintendent and that Kim Nally was calling the law."

"I met her this morning. She seems like a good teacher." I glanced around the room, trying to appear nonchalant, hoping to generate an honest appraisal of her from him.

"She is. Single mother. Her youngster is autistic." He shrugged and wheeled over to his desk where he pushed aside a 35mm Minolta camera and retrieved a pen and pencil can decorated as a scarecrow. "The girl's name is Alicia. She made this for me last Halloween." He turned it over in his hands gently, as if the straw and burlap might bruise. He looked up, his eyes bright. "Kim was proud as punch. She works awful hard for that girl."

"Only child, huh?"

Harper replaced the scarecrow. "Yeah." He spun the chair back to face me and rolled forward. He grimaced when the wheel squeaked. "Gotta get some new bearings." He grinned up at me. "Anyway, that's all I know about that night. I wish I could help you more."

"How well did you know George Holderman?"

He gave an indifferent shrug. "As well as anyone who taught for the guy for five or six years."

"Teachers and staff like him?"

"Some did. Some didn't. Like most superintendents. I never had any dealings with him other than 'hi' or 'bye.' "

His responses smacked of deliberate disinterest. Switching to another subject, I nodded to the bookcase at the end of the blackboard. "How long have you been teaching English?"

"Fifteen-sixteen years. I was out a couple after the accident." He grinned sheepishly and patted his legs. "That's where I got these."

His answer made me slightly uncomfortable. I studied the

books on the shelves. "Hey, here's one of my favorites." I pulled a copy of *A Separate Peace* from the bookrack. "I taught English for a few years at Madison High. Tenth grade. This book I thoroughly enjoyed. One of the few I've read where the first person narrator deliberately lies to the readers."

"A favorite of mine too," he said. "Holden Caulfield is one of my favorite characters."

I frowned, puzzled at his mistake. I started to correct him, but decided against it.

Harper shook his head and gave me a rueful grin. "I'm sorry. I meant Finney. Holden Caulfield is *Catcher in the Rye*. Finney is *A Separate Peace*." He touched his finger to a three-inch scar above his left eye. "Sometimes I forget. I had another accident four years ago on the way to Denver, Colorado. Wrecked my van. I had a fairly long period of retrograde amnesia followed by a year or so of post-traumatic amnesia. I've only been back a couple years." He chuckled. "Even now, I sometimes go blank in the middle of a lecture, but the kids understand."

"Must be tough." I frowned. One accident that paralyzed him, and another from which he suffered amnesia. The guy was an accident waiting to happen.

He arched an eyebrow. "A lot of folks have it a lot tougher." He changed the subject. "You know how Salinger came up with that name, Holden Caulfield, don't you?"

What Salinger groupie didn't know? "Yeah. I heard he was going to a movie starring William Holden and Joan Caulfield. I don't remember the movie's name."

Harper supplied it for me. "*Dear Ruth* in 1947. There was a sequel, *Dear Wife* two years later."

"That's right." I nodded and handed him the book. He took it with his left hand, a reaction I could not fail to notice. "One more question, Mr. Weems."

A look of impatience flickered across his face. "Go on."

"Did Holderman have any enemies that you know of?"

I saw a flash of something in his eyes that he covered so

quickly I couldn't tell if it were surprise or alarm. His reply was hasty and sharp, almost defensive. "Everyone has enemies, Mr. Boudreaux."

I glanced around the room, looking for a subject to calm whatever distress he seemed to be experiencing. My gaze stopped on his camera. "You're a camera buff, huh?"

The tension evaporated instantly. He grinned up at me. "Yeah. I take a lot of the sports pictures for the school paper and the annual. You know anything about photography?"

"Not a bit." I pulled out my notepad and a pen. "Do me a favor. If you don't mind, jot down your name and telephone number right under Kim's in case I need to contact you." I handed him the pad and pen, which he took with his left hand.

I watched with a mixture of elation and confusion as he wrote his name and number with his left hand.

"Here you go." He handed me the pad and pen.

"Thanks." I reached for the door. "Well, look, I appreciate the time, Mr. Weems. That's all I needed to know. I enjoyed the visit."

"Me too."

He looked to me like a good teacher. But something about him bothered me, something besides the left hand. I tried to dismiss it, figuring I was simply uncomfortable because he was handicapped.

After I left his room, I ducked into the boys' restroom. There were no handicapped stalls. I surveyed the room for several seconds, remembering his remark that he had just come out of the restroom when Perry Jacobs reached the bottom of the stairs. "Maybe he just washed his hands," I muttered, shaking my head at my own bad luck. Here I'd found a left-hander, but the only problem was he couldn't have possibly climbed the stairs.

Unless he was faking his condition.

Chapter Eight

On the way to the counselors' office, I stepped outside and called Stewart again. Still no answer. I was growing concerned.

Perry Jacobs was waiting in the counselors' office when I returned. He was about fifty pounds overweight with a flabby face that had once been square. His blond hair was thinning, and his eyes were sad, the brows turned down. He had reached that time in some men's lives when everything sags, his face, his shoulders, his belly, and his dreams. He rose to meet me, hand extended. I apologized for keeping him.

"No problem. I just got here. What's this all about?" He eyed me warily.

I led the way into the ARD room and closed the door behind us. "No big deal, Mr. Jacobs." We sat, and I filled him in on my reason for being there. "So, you see, I'm just going back over information you've already supplied the police."

Instant anger flared in his face. His thick brows met at the bridge of his nose. "I bet," he retorted. He jabbed a finger at me. "You know why Holderman's wife, the little witch, came to you?" His flaccid face was florid with resentment and rage.

Before I could yes, no, or maybe, he continued. "She's trying to dump the blame on anyone except her." He turned to leave. "I'm not staying in here and let some cheap private investigator make me the scapegoat in this thing."

I always expect defensive displays from suspects, but the intensity he exhibited surprised me. I remained seated, hoping to appear calm and unshaken by his diatribe. "Fine with me, Mr. Jacobs. But, understand this. The Safford police gave me permission to open this case again. I figure they'll be curious as to why you don't want to cooperate." I crossed my arms over my chest and stared up at him. "Especially if you don't have anything to hide."

His lips were drawn tightly over clenched teeth. I could almost see the wheels turning in his head.

I gave him a little nudge. "Believe me, I'm accusing no one, but the truth is, the fact your contract was not going to be renewed is a pretty good motive. How old are you, fifty-two? Past that age, jobs, good jobs, aren't easy to come by."

If looks could have killed, I would have been burned to a crispy critter. He placed his hands on the table and leaned forward, resting his weight on his stiff arms. His words were sharp and cold. "For your information, my contract was not going to be denied. George had decided instead to write a letter of reprimand and put it in my file."

I nodded. "That could put a different light on the matter then. Is the letter in your file?"

His tone softened. "No." Wearily, he plopped back down in his chair. "No. We were going to discuss it after the PTA meeting. He was to put the letter in my file the next day." He looked up at me. "I met him in the lobby and walked down the hall with him to my room, but I had to go to the john. He went on up to my room. When I got upstairs, I found him sprawled across my desk." He paused. "And that's the truth, honest." His last words were almost pleading.

"Look, Mr. Jacobs, I know this is tough on you, but if you didn't kill him, then by being completely honest with me, you can help find who did murder George Holderman." I hesitated, hoping my logic would permeate the wall of anger he'd thrown up.

He remained silent. I continued. "Now, back to the contract. I've had experience teaching. I know they can't refuse to renew a contract arbitrarily. What reason did he give for not renewing, or threatening not to renew it?"

He hesitated a moment. "Professional incompetence. In other words, an ineffective teacher. You see, Mr. Boudreaux, a superintendent is god in some of these districts. He has all the records. He can manipulate them anyway he chooses. He appraised me last spring, and he crucified me. He wrote up a remediation plan for me, which I fulfilled this past summer. He came in again last September and literally eviscerated me. That was the basis for the non-renewal."

I stared at him in disbelief. I'd undergone the trauma of teacher appraisals for three or four years at Madison High, and they were always done by the teacher's immediate supervisor, the principal. "Why did he appraise you? I'd figure Howard Birnam, your principal, would do that."

With a cynical chuckle, he explained, "Holderman claimed he liked to keep his hand in things.' In fairness to him, he usually appraised several teachers on various campuses each year. Said it helped him keep up with what was going on in the district."

"Why would he hit on you and not the others?"

Perry Jacobs hesitated once again, then shrugged. "He never liked me. And the feeling was reciprocated."

I considered his explanation. Hard to believe, but having been in the school business, I knew for a fact there were many vindictive school administrators who would not hesitate to fire an employee on a whim or in an egotistical display of power.

For the moment, I dropped the subject and jotted a few notes in my notebook. "Kim Nally said you saw someone going down the stairs that night."

"Naw. I didn't." He shook his head. "I came up the middle flight of stairs. When I turned the corner toward my room, I thought I caught a glimpse of someone going down the far stairs. I didn't think anything about it until I saw George. About that time, Kim came up. I remembered seeing someone, or thinking I had. I told Kim to call nine-one-one, and I ran down the stairs."

"Find anyone?"

Frustration clouded his eyes. "Harp Weems."

A flicker of hope erased the frustration in his eyes. "But, you can check with Jim Hawkins. He teaches American History next door to me. He came into the boys' room just before I left. He can back me up that I was in there while George had gone on to my room." A pleased smile played over his fleshy face.

"Did Hawkins see Holderman going up the stairs?"

His grin faded. He stared at me a moment, puzzled.

I explained. "You could have gone up there with Holderman, killed him, then hurried back to the boys' room where you saw your friend, which provided part of an alibi. I'm not saying you did, but that's how the cops might look at it."

With a rueful twist of his lips, he nodded. "Yeah. I see what you mean. But, I am telling the truth."

The shrill shriek of the school bell interrupted us. He rose quickly. "I've got a class."

I stood with him. "Look, Mr. Jacobs. I'd still like to talk a little more. Can I get in touch with you at home?"

He studied me a moment. With a weary shake of his head, he chuckled. "Sure. If I got to, I got to. Perry Jacobs. I'm in the Austin directory, on Canyon Road. Four seventy-six."

I slid a sheet of paper to him. "How about writing it down for me?"

A frown wrinkled his forehead, but he just shrugged. "Whatever." Hurriedly, he scribbled his address, with his right hand and handed it to me.

Hiding my disappointment, I took the address. "Thanks."

I offered him my hand but he ignored it. He stared hard at me, his gray eyes challenging. "Make sure you look hard at that wife of George's. She was here. I can always find another teaching job, even substituting if I have to. She can't find another eight million."

Noncommittally, I replied, "I will."

"Good."

I studied his retreating back. He was right. He could find another job, but Frances Holderman couldn't find another eight million.

Chapter Nine

The next period, I interviewed Dorothy Saussy who verified being with Kim Nally. She insisted she left Nally's room with Linda May and Iona Flores precisely at nine-thirty.

The other names on the list were of no help. Henry Bishop, the government teacher, and Lionel Portis, the Driver's Ed instructor, contributed nothing. They had been in Bishop's room planning the next student council meeting. Jim Hawkins verified seeing Perry Jacobs in the boys' room, but when I asked if he had seen Holderman climbing the stairs, he shook his head, which was bad news for Jacobs.

Afterward, despite the chill in the air, I strolled the campus, locating the auditorium where the PTA meeting had been held and studying its proximity to Room 247. Tall shrubs lined the building, and from the front door of the auditorium to the side door leading to Room 247 was a straight shot, less than seventy-five yards across the quadrangle.

I did some fast calculating.

Two minutes through the dark night, two minutes upstairs, two minutes to whack Holderman, two minutes back down, and two minutes to the auditorium. Ten minutes. A flicker of time in the commotion of two hundred chattering people clustered in the auditorium lobby.

The perp would not be missed, and by cutting across the quadrangle, he could bypass the sign-in sheet kept by the hall monitors.

I finished the morning by interviewing the hall monitors, two husky young men about three or four inches taller than my five-ten, Tim Briggs and Marvin Handwell, whom the high school principal had assigned to monitor the old wing.

Any parent would have been proud to claim either young man as a son. Polite and good-looking, they both carried the bulk of a football player. They greeted me and waited until I offered them a chair. I explained my reason for being there and slid the sign-in sheet across the desk. "As I understand it, you two young men were hall monitors that night. Here's the list of teachers who went into that wing. Is it complete?"

Tim Briggs, broad shoulders with red hair and freckles, picked up the list and read the names. "Kim Nally, Perry Jacobs, George Holderman, Harper Weems, Jim Hawkins, Dorothy Saussy, Henry Bishop, Linda May, Iona Flores, and Lionel Portis." The boys looked at each other. Marvin nodded to Tim.

"Yes, sir, Mr. Boudreaux," Tim replied, handing me the list. "As close as I can remember, this was all who went into that wing. Mr. Birnam had us sit in front of the first stairway in that wing. No one could have gone in or out without passing in front of us."

I took the list. I couldn't help noticing the expensive gold watch on his wrist and the matching gold ring on his other hand. "Hey, nice looking ring."

Both boys held out their hands, showing the massive gold rings on their ring fingers. Marvin grinned at me. "Yes, sir. Our senior rings. Twelve years we worked for them."

The setting was blue, one of the school colors. I chided the boys. "I'm surprised your girlfriends don't have them."

Both boys laughed. Tim nodded. "My girl's hinted at it. I might give it to her."

Marvin snorted. "Not me, man. At least, not now. Maybe after we switch them."

"Switch them?" I frowned. "What's that?"

Tim explained. "A Safford High School tradition, Mr. Boudreaux. When we graduate, we shift the ring from the left ring finger to the right one as a symbol of graduation."

"Yeah," Marvin echoed. "Just like switching the tassels on our mortar boards."

I grinned. "Well, boys. Good luck." I held up the list. "Tell me, Do you know Fred Seebell or Frances Holderman?"

Marvin Handwell wore a mushroom haircut. "I know Mrs. Holderman, but, ah, you know, not that guy."

"Did you see her that night?"

"No, sir." Marvin shook his head. He leaned back and crossed his heavily muscled arms across his broad chest.

"I did," replied Tim. "She was in the lobby."

"But, in the hall, Tim. Did she come down the hall?"

"No." He indicated the list of names in my hand. "Only the ones on that list went down the hall."

The boys looked at each other. Marvin nodded.

"You boys still monitor the halls?"

Tim nodded. "Yes, sir. Whenever Mr. Birnam asks. You see, some of the PTA parents bring their children. Mr. Birnam, he just wants to keep the kids out of the halls."

"So, he gets you football players, huh?"

The boys blushed. Marvin shrugged. "Well, not exactly because of football. We play football, but, we're both in the National Honor Society. That's the group Mr. Birnam uses to monitor the halls."

"One more question. Iona Flores and Linda May. How long were they in the wing?" If the two had just entered the wing to pick up Dorothy Saussy, they should have returned shortly.

Tim frowned. "It's been a long time, Mr. Boudreaux."

"I know. But, think. Give it a try."

Marvin chewed on his bottom lip. "It wasn't long before they came back out with Mrs. Saussy. She teaches algebra too."

Tim agreed. "Yes, sir. Mrs. Flores was my Algebra Two teacher. She's a real good teacher too. Marvin never had her, and while they were gone, I told him about her. They were back before I could finish."

I studied them. Maybe if the kids in my English classes back at Madison High School had been like these two, I'd still be teaching. "Thanks, boys. You can go on back to class now."

Turning down Howard Birnam's offer for lunch in the cafeteria, I left the building and headed for my pickup, not once regretting my refusal of his offer. I reminded myself that with public school, college, and then six years teaching behind me, I'd had enough school lunches to last me a lifetime. But the truth was, I was anxious to get back to the apartment to check on Stewart.

Chapter Ten

I hesitated when I reached my pickup. A folded slip of paper was under the windshield wiper. Glancing around, I retrieved it and popped it open. The note inside was succinct: BACK OFF.

I whistled softly and glanced around. I already had someone's attention. Slipping the note into my shirt pocket, I climbed in and slammed the door. I was anxious to check on Stewart.

Less than three blocks from the school, the rear of my pickup swayed, and then I heard the chilling flop, flop, flop of a flat tire. I pulled up in front of a convenience store and climbed out. Both rear tires were flat. "What the . . ."

Disgusted, I aimed a kick at a deflated tire, wondering just what I had run over. I had one spare. One spare and two flats don't calculate out right. Cursing, I called my auto club. While waiting for road service, I tried my home number again, and again, no answer. "Stewart, where the dickens are you?"

Fifteen minutes later, a wrecker from Riverside Salvage pulled up, hoisted the rear of my truck off the ground, and quickly repaired the flats. Both had been punctured by two-inch roofing nails. And to make the incident even more curious, each puncture was between the two middle treads of the tire.

The driver of the wrecker looked up at me, then glanced in the direction of the high school. A grin split his round face. "You a teacher?"

I shook my head.

He shrugged. "Well, I don't know, friend, but it looks like to me someone was playing a trick on you."

I glanced back down the road toward the high school. A trick? Or a warning?

I groaned when I drew near my apartment. Stewart's Pontiac was gone. "Jeez, Tony. Now what? Some family you are. Your ward hasn't been here twenty-four hours and already you've lost him. I sure hope Leroi doesn't call," I muttered, pulling into the drive. "Just take it easy," I mumbled, trying to reassure myself. "The boy'll be in later." But, I was worried sick.

Inside, my fears vanished. Stewart had taped a note to my computer. He was being interviewed for a job and would be home by five or six. I sighed with relief and wandered into the kitchen where I almost stepped on an empty milk saucer. Stewart must have fed the kitten. I looked through the apartment, but the tiny gray kitten was nowhere to be seen.

Giving up my search, I plopped down in front of the computer and began transcribing my notes, placing a copy in the new file I created on my hard drive, a copy on a disk, and then printing up two hard copies, one for me, and one for Marty.

The remainder of the afternoon flew past. When I finished around five-thirty or so, I rose, stretched, and peered out the window. Outside, dusk crept over the neighborhood like a sly cat, soundless on its padded feet.

Returning to my computer, I studied my notes. While I hadn't found too much that wasn't in the police report, what I did learn from the interviews engendered some fascinating theories.

Kim Nally had an abortion about which she had said nothing. Could it be the result of a scandal threatened by Frances Holderman?

Then came Perry Jacobs' assertion that Holderman decided to issue a reprimand instead of denying a contract. First, I wanted to verify the claim that Holderman appraised teachers, which while there was nothing wrong with it, was unusual. On the other hand, I found it difficult to believe anyone would take away another's livelihood just because of dislike. But then, we were talking about administrative educators, many of whom are not members of the intelligentsia.

I looked up abruptly when a car door slammed. Moments later, Stewart burst in with a big grin on his face. He waved as he headed for the bathroom. "Gotta hurry, Tony. I got the job, and my boss is taking me out to dinner tonight. Hope you weren't planning anything," he blurted out before I had a chance to say a word.

I had figured on the two of us going out for dinner, but I just shook my head. "No. Nothing. What kind of job is it?"

"I start off doing delivery work. Austin Expediters is the name of the company," he replied, and through the open bathroom door, he gave a running description of his day while he showered and dressed. He was a nice looking young man. About six feet, well-built, and when he flashed that bright smile, his brilliant white teeth contrasted sharply with his café au lait-colored skin.

As quickly as he breezed in, he stormed out. "Back around ten or so!" he shouted, slamming the door.

"Hey, wait," I jumped up and yanked open the door. "How can I get in touch with you if I have to?"

He opened the door of his car and paused. "My cell," and called out the number. He grinned and slid into the Pontiac. "See you later," he called out the window as he sped away.

I watched until the blue Pontiac turned the corner. At least, he was all right, and I had a cell number. I picked up the phone and called Leroi, bringing him up to date on his son.

Hanging up, I decided to splurge on a thick T-bone and a bottle of fine red wine out at the Old San Francisco Steak House on I-35.

Sorry AA. I'll try again tomorrow.

And splurge I did with baked potato smothered with butter, heaped with sour cream and sprinkled with crisp bacon. Homemade hot rolls soaked with butter. And a succulent steak two inches thick. All washed down with fruity red wine.

I didn't consider myself a gourmet even in the loosest definition of the word, but that night, I caught a fleeting glimmer of the poetry of good food and wine of which the very rich always speak. In the next instant, my newfound hedonistic appetite for Epicurean delights vanished when Janice Coffman-Morrison and a broad-shouldered blond right out of *Gentlemans' Quarterly* walked in. As much as I hate to admit it, he carried himself with the casual aplomb of the very rich and spoiled.

Wearing a black dinner dress with a necklace of diamonds the size of ping-pong balls, Janice paused in the entrance and purposely surveyed the room. Her gaze settled on me, and with a faint smile, she glided in my direction. Gentleman Quarterly followed. Like a puppy, I told myself, not the least bit jealous. Not much. I felt my ears tingle.

Obviously, she'd spotted my Silverado pickup outside. Not surprising for among Lexuses, Jaguars, Mercedes, and Luminas, my truck stuck out.

She paused at my table. "Hello, Tony," she said imperiously.

I rose, affecting a casual aplomb of my own. "Why, Janice. How are you?"

"Wonderful." She half turned and held out her hand to her new beau. "This is Nelson Vanderweg. Of the Montreal Vanderwegs. He just drove in from Dallas."

"Nelson." I extended my hand, noting the sharp pleat in his dark slacks and the easy drape of his jacket over his narrow hips.

"I've heard much of you, Mr. Boudreaux." His tone was flat

and without emotion. On his face was an expression of pained haughtiness.

I replied with a nod, then turned to Janice. "How have you been?"

She beamed and linked both her arms through Nelson's. "Wonderful," she exclaimed, hugging his arm to her.

"Good."

Nelson coughed.

A couple of awkward moments passed as the three of us stared at each other, no one knowing exactly what to say. I decided to make an effort to be gracious. "Would you and Janice care to join me, Nelson?"

He tilted his chin slightly. "No, thank you. We have reservations." His words were polite, but his tone was brazen with contempt.

Despite the urge to stick out my tongue at them, I smiled. "You two have a good time," I said, stepping aside so they could pass.

Janice giggled. "We will."

I glared at Nelson's retreating back. "And I hope you choke," I muttered under my breath, shedding my newly found casual aplomb for redneck hostility.

Naturally, my relaxing evening of gastronomic delights was ruined. I shrugged off my thin veneer of the very rich and reverted to my redneck ways by demanding a doggie bag so I could take the remainder of my meal with me. The half-full bottle of red wine, I stuck in my jacket pocket.

The maitre d', his upper lip stiff, eyed the bottle in my jacket pocket with disdain and contempt. I was half a breath away from grabbing the neck of the bottle and smashing that sneering little cretin across the bridge of his hooked nose. But I refrained, displaying what I thought was magnificent self-control.

The sky was clear, the stars bright, and the temperature had plunged. A puff of frost edged my breath. I paused before climbing in my Chevy Silverado and stared at the gaudy façade of the steakhouse, my frustration with Janice still simmering. I drew a deep breath and reminded myself that the very rich view life far differently than the average working stiff.

For some reason, I thought of Frances Holderman. Perry Jacobs had raised a couple of salient points. She could have ducked out the front door and, hidden by the darkness, slipped across the quadrangle, and then upstairs. And she had two dandy motives. Not only had she been the betrayed wife, but also the beneficiary of eight million bucks.

But how did she come up with the ball bat? The teachers could have hidden one in their room, but she had no room, which meant she had to carry it with her.

Unlike a switchblade that could be hidden anywhere, the only place she could have concealed it was under her skirt, a next-to-impossible feat if the skin tightskirt she wore at our initial meeting was her choice of dress. On the other hand, perhaps she had secreted it in the shrubbery by the door.

I turned off the freeway, hoping Stewart was home.

Chapter Eleven

Its wary yellow eyes watching my every move, the kitten was the only one waiting for me.

Stopping in the kitchen doorway, I glared at the tiny thing. "You think you got me beat, don't you? Well, you don't," I added, striding into the kitchen.

I nuked some more milk, then opened the bottle of red wine, stuck the doggie bag in the microwave, and plopped down in front of my computer. I tried to concentrate on formulating a list of questions for Frances Holderman and Fred Seebell, whose wife had been George Holderman's mistress before Kim Nally took her place, but Stewart remained on the fringes of my thoughts.

I glanced at my cell phone, wondering if I should call Stewart. I shrugged off the notion. "Come on, Tony. The boy's twenty-two. He can take care of himself." Despite my worry, I forced myself to concentrate on the job at hand.

Just like Frances Holderman, Seebell could have slipped out of the lobby and whacked Holderman. Either could have stashed the bat in the shrubs by the door, and either could have plunged the switchblade into Holderman's heart.

Of course, I faced the same dead end confronted by the

Safford police. Neither Frances Holderman nor Fred Seebell were left-handed. At least, according to the police report.

"Wait a minute," I muttered, holding the wine glass at my lips, as an idea popped into my head. "Could any of the suspects be ambidextrous?" I hesitated, wondering if the department had considered such a possibility.

Excited, I booted up the disk Chief Pachuca had given me containing all three hundred and eighty pages of evidence. Utilizing the FIND command, I searched for *ambidextrous*. Nowhere did I find it.

I considered the matter. Crime scene analysis is only as good as the technician interpreting the evidence. To one tech, a piece of physical evidence might take on one meaning, to another, an entirely different significance. Often, after the analysis and synthesis of the evidence, the theory can take a skew completely contrary to initial concepts.

Going back to the FIND command, I searched for the word, evidence, pausing at each recognition to read the pertinent sentences. Suddenly, I found myself staring at a list of personal evidence taken from the desk of George Holderman, which was contained in a box in the evidence room at Safford police station. Skimming down the list, I saw nothing unusual until I reached his desk pad, that ubiquitous business tool found on ninety percent of the desks in this country. The typical desk pad is a calendar, appointment pad, doodle pad, holiday reminder, and calculating pad.

Continuing through the disk, I found no other reference to the desk pad. I paused, staring at the monitor, remembering how I used my own desk pad at the office. Could Holderman have made a reference to Perry Jacobs on the pad? A note, a reminder to write a letter of reprimand? If such a note existed, Perry Jacobs could be eliminated as a suspect, which, while it would not solve the case, would cut the list of suspects by one.

Maybe Perry Jacobs' display of anger during the interview was actually a legitimate exhibition of righteous indignation. Regardless, he had raised some questions about Frances

Holderman, questions whose answers could prove quite interesting.

I don't care who does the slicing or how thin they slice the bread, you'll always end up with two sides. Perhaps Perry Jacobs' theory about the other side of the bread had some merit. Of all the suspects other than Jacobs, Frances Holderman had the most compelling of motives.

I spent a few minutes trying to decide how to approach Frances Holderman. I wanted to know if she had indeed been aware of Nally's abortion, and if, as Rita Viator had said, she swore scandal unless Nally aborted. I hesitated, my fingers resting on the keyboard. I decided to do some background on her.

Going online, I found nothing.

On impulse, I decided to see what I could find out about Janice's newfound companion, Nelson Vanderweg. Of the Montreal Vanderwegs, I reminded myself.

To my surprise, a Vanderweg wasn't listed in Montreal. I tried the remaining six of my white page databases. Again no matches. In fact, I couldn't find a Vanderweg in all of Quebec.

I chuckled. "Maybe they were run out of town," I muttered, taking a perverse delight in the thought, at the same time experiencing a tinge of guilt for the guy had done nothing to me. For several more seconds, I stared at the monitor, puzzled. I continued staring at the screen, speculating. Did Janice say Montreal? No question at all about that. She spit it out at me like it was an Academy Award or Grammy.

So, why wasn't there a Vanderweg in Montreal? One of two explanations. Either she had misunderstood or he lied to her. I discounted the misunderstanding, for he was at her side when she introduced us. He heard her, and he could have corrected her at the time.

But he didn't.

Something smelled. And it wasn't bad fish.

I glanced at my watch. Twelve-twenty. Stewart was late. I couldn't help wondering if he'd had an accident. Or—

The jangling of the phone interrupted my misgivings. It was Stewart. He was spending the night with a friend. A soft voice in the background told me all I needed to know. I glanced at the caller ID for a phone number. "Okay, Stewart. Take care. See you tomorrow. By the way, give your dad a call, you hear?"

"Right away, Tony. Count on it."

After he hung up, I did a reverse check on the number and secured an address, 314 Festival Beach Street. And I'm not ashamed to admit, I planned to see if he was indeed there. And I was also jealous enough that I might just check on Janice.

I grabbed a leftover beer from the refrigerator, then on second thought put it back. I'd trampled too many of my AA vows the last few hours. Time to make amends, so I grabbed a soft drink instead.

To my relief, Stewart's Pontiac was where it was supposed to be, parked in front of 314 Festival Beach Street, so I drove over to Janice's condo on the Colorado River despite the hour. A black E-Class, E55 AMG Mercedes coupe was parked behind her Miata. I eased past, but it was too dark to make out the license number.

Turning around at the end of the block, I headed back. When I reached her drive, I turned in, then quickly backed out, heading in the direction from which I had come. If they spotted the headlights, they would figure it was simply someone turning around.

But in those couple of seconds, I memorized his license number. It was a Texas number, which meant either he had played the conscientious citizen and registered immediately upon moving to the state, or else he'd been in the state since the last license renewal.

I parked around the corner and waited, planning on finding out just where Nelson Vanderweg called home. I leaned back and waited.

The long day caught up with me. When I jerked awake at four o'clock, the Mercedes had vanished. All that was left for me to do was mutter a few curses and go back to my place.

Chapter Twelve

I'd slept enough in my pickup that I was wide awake when I passed I HOP on Lamar Boulevard. I pulled into the takeout window and waited as they packaged me hot cakes, fried eggs, peppered sausage, blackberry syrup, and a pint of coffee, a Cajun's concept of a heart healthy breakfast.

Nelson Vanderweg had me wired. I had to know more about him. Call it ego, which it was, but even though he was better looking than me, and richer, and probably more sensitive to a woman's needs, and undoubtedly a better dancer, and displayed better manners, I didn't feel as if he deserved Janice as much as I did.

And to be truthful, that admission surprised me, for after my wife, Diane, and I divorced, I never seriously considered marriage, not even with Janice. Yet, now, here I was, jealous, the scorned lover.

Opening my breakfast tray, I placed it beside my computer and booted the machine. Eat and compute. I glanced at the clock. Almost five. That gave me about three hours.

I felt something rubbing my ankle and then a faint meow. I glared at the kitten, which seemed to be putting on a little weight. It stopped rubbing and looked up at me, purring softly.

"All right," I groused, at the same time tearing off half the sausage and dropping it on the carpet at the kitten's feet. "Here."

Then I went to work. First I looked up the E-Class, E55 AMG Mercedes. A 2005 model, it invoiced at over $75,000. I stared at the picture on the screen, trying to imagine the feeling of climbing behind the wheel of such a vehicle.

With a shake of my head, I searched all my databases for Nelson Vanderweg. The minutes turned into an hour, then two. Nothing. Before I knew it, my breakfast tray was empty, my coffee cold, and my eyes burning. I dumped the empty containers, showered and shaved, and headed for the office.

My next step was the Texas Motor Vehicle Registry disks Marty updated yearly. I crossed my fingers that Vanderweg's license was listed. If he'd registered the vehicle with a new license since the publication of the current registry, I'd be out of luck.

Marty puffed in just as I pulled up the program. Red-faced, he glanced at the screen, then looked away. "How's the Holderman business going?" He was breathing hard.

"Moving on. Finish with Seebell and Holderman today, but I've got some background I want to look at." I didn't tell him I was doing some personal research on his time.

He removed his topcoat and hat, poured some coffee, and plopped across the desk from me. The chair groaned. "Anything substantial?" He blew on his coffee and sipped at it gingerly. He sighed in pleasure. "Coffee's good." A gust of wind rattled the window. He shivered. "Especially on a lousy day like today."

"Yeah," I muttered, scanning the registry for the license number.

At that moment, Al Grogan came in, a large, beefy man with the intuitive perception of Sherlock Holmes. Hey, as far as I knew, he might be a descendent of the fictional gumshoe. Al poured some coffee and headed for his nook. To my relief, Marty followed.

Then I found the license number. That was the good news. The bad news was that it was registered to Clarence Jolly in Amarillo, Texas, several hundred miles north. I jotted down his address, then looking over my shoulder to make sure Marty was not standing behind me, I punched in *67 and then placed a call to Amarillo.

The phone picked up on the second ring. A stiff, cool voice answered. "Jolly residence."

"Clarence Jolly?" I heard a muffled voice in the background.

"Yes, but he isn't in," she replied curtly. "Would you care to leave a message?"

I could visualize a pinch-lipped shrew in a maid's uniform taking orders from the voice in the background. I wasn't going to get anywhere with her by normal channels. So, I decided to stir up some excitement in Amarillo. "Yes. Tell him this is Ed George of George's Wrecking Yard in Austin. I got Jolly's Mercedes down here and I want to know where to send the bill. He owes two thousand bucks for storage."

There was a moment of silence at the other end, and then I heard muffled voices. I grinned, imagining the scene. Clarence Jolly was probably gaping at her in disbelief.

Abruptly, a belligerent voice came over the line. "What do you think you're talking about, buddy? I sold that Mercedes."

"You Clarence Jolly?"

"Yeah. But I don't own that Mercedes."

I continued my lie. "Sorry, bud. According to the up-to-date registry, you own it. We got it in storage and you owe two grand on it."

He muttered a curse. "Look . . . who are you?"

"Ed George. I own George's Wrecking and Towing down here in Austin. Cops had me haul this black Mercedes E-Fifty-five AMG off the street. I want to know who's paying for it. You're listed as the owner."

His voice became placating. "Look, Mr. George. I sold that car three weeks ago to a guy out of Boulder, Colorado. His name was Nelson Villafono. Some kind of Greek, I guess. I don't even know what Villafono is, but he wrote me a check on a Boulder bank. It cleared without a problem. After it did, I signed the title over to him. He's the one you need to get hold of. I don't want to get involved in this. It ain't none of my business now."

"Don't know if I can keep you out of it or not, Mr. Jolly. Somebody's got to pay the fee. Can you tell me anything about him so I can track him down?"

"I don't know much about him. He hung around here a few days. Said he had some business to take care of. He even paid for my call to his bank."

"Where'd he stay? Any idea?"

"No. Wait a minute. Yeah, yeah. He said something about staying at the Ranchmans' Motel out on Highway Sixty, the Pampa highway. They might be able to tell you where he was headed." He hesitated, then gave an embarrassed laugh. "Sorry. You already know that. You got his car. He must've gone to Austin from here."

I thanked Clarence Jolly and hung up. For several moments I stared at the receiver trying to focus my thoughts. I had a couple of options with Nelson Villafono or Vanderweg or whatever. The fastest would be to check the arrest records in Boulder. I jotted a reminder in my notebook, and then headed for the door.

Before I visited Perry Jacobs again, I wanted to see George Holderman's desk pad, which was being held in the evidence room at Safford Police Station. If Jacobs was telling the truth about the letter or reprimand, maybe I could find some mention of it on the pad.

The wind had dropped, but the sky remained cloudy, keeping the temperature in the low forties.

* * *

That George Holderman was a meticulous person was evident. My own desk pad was a collage of indecipherable doodles, upside down notes, scribbled reminders, vague questions, and some drawings that could be labeled marginally obscene. Holderman's notes were in precise hand and confined to the respective boxes. As each obligation was met, he placed a checkmark beside it. Once all obligations for the day were met, a neat X crossed off the box.

The last box X'ed out was Monday, November 10, 2004. November 11 was the night he was murdered, and one of the notations in the box was to see PJ. In parentheses beside the note was written a name and business, AW, CR Real Estate.

PJ? AW? CR? I skimmed the previous days. Some names were written, some abbreviated. PJ? Could that be Perry Jacobs? My pulse quickened. Perry and a real estate agent in the same note? I glanced back over the November calendar. Each of Holderman's appointments were numbered, neatly separating one meeting from the other. If this AW was a separate appointment, Holderman would have indicated such.

On my own desk pad, my notes were so confused that at times I couldn't figure out what I was supposed to do. But not Holderman. Talk about organized. I hated organized people.

I could almost reprise his day on an hour-by-hour basis, both personal and professional. Quickly, I thumbed through the yellow pages for real estate and discovered one CR, Colorado River Real Estate, owner, Al Waldron.

Bingo. AW.

I jotted down Al Waldron's address and phone number.

Skimming back over November, I saw no commentary regarding a letter of reprimand for Jacobs. I looked for the previous months' records. They were nowhere around. I checked with the officer in charge. He frowned at the cream-colored pad. "Yeah. I remember. There's a whole box full of them pages. Folded in quarters and stuck in brown envelopes. Guess the guy saved them for whatever reason."

I suppressed a grin. Having been in the school business, I knew why Holderman saved everything—to cover his tail from irate parents upset because their precious child had to stay after school or didn't make the cheerleading squad or any of another number of reasons, none of them having to do with class work.

The box of envelopes turned out to be a gold mine of information. My initial inspection was cursory because of the detail, and I quickly realized that even if Holderman had kept a diary, he could not have provided more information than did the years of notes.

And he was as meticulous in archiving them as keeping them. Each sheet, eighteen inches by fifteen, was folded into neat quarters, and placed in manila envelopes with the year written in felt-tip on the outside. Twelve years' worth. The job would take me hours.

Safford Police Chief Billy Vanbiber let me sign for the box of Holderman's notes. "Thanks, Chief. I'll have them back in a couple of days, if that's okay with you."

He gave me a big grin. "Chief Pachuca said you're okay. Take your time."

Sometimes the good old boy network pays off.

Chapter Thirteen

Colorado River Real Estate was on the way back to my place on Peyton-Gin Road, so I decided to stop by.

Al Waldron did not look like a real estate salesman, which was probably why he was so successful. A short, rotund man with close-clipped, neatly combed hair, he wore a genial smile and his warm tone instantly convinced you that you were the most important person in the world.

His demeanor didn't even crack when I identified myself as a private investigator. He simply ushered me into an office with expansive windows offering a sweeping overlook of the Colorado River, a wide ribbon of gray water below. The room was tastefully appointed, but not ostentatious.

The only time the smile fled his face was when I explained that I was looking into Holderman's death. Al shook his head. "Shame about that. George Holderman was a good man. He was a risk-taker. He almost made the big time."

"The big time? You mean, in real estate?"

"That's where the money is today." He eyed me curiously. "You ever been tempted to take a flier, take a risk? I know where there's some speculative property for a fair price. If the right things happen in the next couple years, a man could spend the rest of his days on the French Riveria sipping Dom Perignon and eating Beluga Caviar."

"What kind of caviar?"

"Beluga Caviar. The best. Hey, one sturgeon can carry up to several thousand dollars worth of caviar."

"I've heard of caviar, but not that Beluga stuff."

He grinned. "Top of the line caviar. Straight out of the Caspian Sea. A hundred and fifty bucks an ounce. Now, what about it? Want to take a chance?"

I made a face, then laughed. "On what I make? You'd run me out of here if you knew what I take home weekly."

He joined the laughter, but kept selling. "George started small. He did everything the right way. He saved, invested as he could. Never lost patience or hope. Almost had it. You probably could do the same thing."

Now I was seeing another side of Holderman, though his strong appetite for life and his meticulous attention to detail seemed to fit right in with his investment strategies. "What happened?"

Waldron's smile faded. He paused and stared into the air over my head. "Too often, Mr. Boudreaux, all of the careful planning, the well thought out strategies, blow up because of one factor." He fixed his eyes on mine. "Greed."

I frowned. "Greed? You mean he lost his money?"

Waldron nodded. "Not all of it, about half. And on top of that, he made himself one big enemy."

My pulse raced. An enemy? Who could Waldron be talking about? My brain raced. The only name I could come up with was Perry Jacobs. "Go on. He listened to the wrong person, you said. Who? Who is the enemy he made?"

He hesitated.

"Look, Mr. Waldron. Holderman's dead. I don't know if whoever you're talking about had anything to do with it or not, but it could be important."

He gave me a sheepish grin. "I always figured it could, Mr.

Boudreaux, but when the police never came to ask questions, I dismissed it. If they didn't think it was important, why should I?"

I'm always amazed at just how easy it is for people to lie to themselves so they won't have to be involved. It's so much more comfortable to simply forget about a bad situation if possible. Push it out of your mind. Let someone else handle it.

But, I bit my tongue. I still needed information, so I couldn't alienate the man. "I don't know, Mr. Waldron. Could be they knew nothing about Holderman's real estate interests."

He shrugged. "Maybe." A tinge of embarrassment colored his plump cheeks.

"So, who is this enemy you're talking about?"

He hesitated. "Maybe enemy is too strong a word."

I was growing impatient. "Come on, Waldron. Either you tell me, or I'll bring the cops out. I don't have time for games."

An embarrassed grin spread over his round face. "I'm sorry, Mr. Boudreaux." He gave a deep sigh. "Look, Boudreaux, I'm like most. I don't want to get involved."

"I understand. But, you understand, you might have information that will help find the killer. Either way, Mr. Waldron, you're going to give us the information you have."

He nodded. "I know."

"Good. Now, this enemy he made. Who is it? The same one who told him about the investment?"

"No. Chu Cheng Lee talked George into investing. We all thought the deal was legitimate, so George convinced a friend to invest. This friend did and lost it all. They almost went to blows right here in this office."

"Who is the friend?"

Waldron hesitated.

"Come on, Waldron. Who are we talking about?"

"Perry Jacobs," he replied softly. "Perry Jacobs is the man who lost everything."

My reply was couched in the archetypical Tony Boudreaux eloquence. "P . . . P . . . Perry Jacobs?"

He nodded.

"The teacher? The schoolteacher? That Perry Jacobs? He lost everything?" Motive in capital letters flashed before my eyes. Compound that with his loss of a contract, and you could be talking lethal injection time. But then I reminded myself that a teacher couldn't have that much to lose anyway.

Again, Waldron nodded. Clearing his throat, he explained. "Chu Cheng Lee set up a parent corporation to invest in several large real estate complexes in and around Austin. He was smooth. Half a dozen Chinese nationals invested over twelve million with him. At first, the investments paid off nicely for Holderman. At the time, him and Jacobs were on friendly terms. Jacobs laughed at Holderman when he heard about the investment. Said Holderman was a sucker, but when Holderman picked up a nicc little thirty percent return on his investment the first year, Jacobs jumped in. He sold the old family property on the other side of Lake Travis and followed Holderman's advice. He sunk his entire savings in the scheme."

I changed the thrust of the conversation slightly. "What about you? You get in on it?"

"At first, then I got out. Something about Chu Lee bothered me. I tried to talk to Holderman about it, but he refused to listen even though we had worked together for years in various investment strategies."

Waldron shook his head at the frown on my face. "It turned out to be the old pyramid scheme, Mr. Boudreaux. We later learned that Lee had carefully constructed a paper empire, complete with slick brochures picturing the brand new Alamo Life Insurance Building in downtown Austin, which he claimed he owned. In addition, he convinced his investors he was in the process of purchasing eight or ten Fortune Five hundred companies. In the beginning, he had a world-class center of operations for the whole world to see. For a couple years, he floated fraudulent loans with which to pay off investors and draw in more money."

"And that's how Holderman made his thirty percent?"

Waldron chuckled. "Part of the game. He was one of Chu Cheng Lee's shills. Unknowingly, of course. Lee paid off handsomely for the first couple years to three or four of his initial investors." He chuckled ruefully. "Like they say, hindsight is twenty-twenty. Anyway, most investors, like Perry Jacobs, were greedy. They sunk all their profits back into the scheme. The exceptional dividends drew in more suckers. Money poured in. Then, just before the whole scheme crashed about him, Chu Cheng Lee closed out the accounts and headed for no-one-knows-where, probably some exotic island where the USA has no extradition treaties."

Unlike some who can maintain layers of complex, contradictory stratagems and intrigues, I have never been able to think in intricate and convoluted schemes. I'm a simple person, and I think simply, which is one of the reasons I'm still number seven on Marty's list of employees. Of course, we only have seven PIs on the payroll. My next question echoed my simple thinking. "So Jacobs blamed Holderman?"

Waldron arched an eyebrow. "You got it."

"But, what about Holderman? Didn't he lose his investment also?"

A wry grin played over his face. "I'm no philosopher, Mr. Boudreaux. I'm just a plain door-to-door salesman who has had a little luck come his way. A lot of things happen in this world that I don't understand. But I know that at times, fate steps in and throws me a curve, and turns around and lobs you one right down the middle that you knock out of the park. That's the way life is."

I had to agree.

He continued. "That's what happened. Holderman pulled out before the scheme folded. I don't know how he knew, or if he knew. Maybe it was just a hunch. Maybe he decided to listen to me. I don't know. But, from what I heard, he tried to talk Jacobs into pulling out also."

I grimaced. “Maybe Holderman was in it with Lee.”

Waldron shrugged. “Maybe. I don’t think so. Of course, Jacobs swore he was. Like I told you, they almost came to blows in this office. And Jacobs threatened to kill Holderman.”

“You heard Perry Jacobs threaten George Holderman’s life?”

The rotund salesman chewed on his bottom lip thoughtfully. “Actually, he said ‘I’ll get you.’ Now, take that to mean whatever you want.”

“What about Lee’s records? That might indicate Holderman’s culpability.” I knew the answer but I wanted to hear it said.

“Forget it.” Waldron nodded to the south. “Lee destroyed all records before he skipped. There’s no indication of how much Holderman made or lost. All I know is when he pulled out, he claimed he’d lost half of his investment. If you have to know for sure, there’s always tax records. He’s bound to have filed a return.”

“I agree. But, he might not.”

“Yeah.” He laughed. “By the way, are you sure you wouldn’t be interested in a sound little investment? I could almost guarantee a handsome profit. All legitimate.”

I shook my head. “No, thanks. One other question. Holderman was killed on November 11. He and Jacobs were to meet with you that day.”

Waldron raised his eyebrows. “They did. That morning. That was when they almost came to blows.”

“How can you be sure of the date?”

“I read about his death in the paper the next day.”

Chapter Fourteen

A chilling drizzle began falling as I pulled away from the real estate agency. Putting off my visit to Seebell and Holderman, I pulled onto I-35 and headed north. Fifteen minutes later, I pulled into the drive at my apartment and lugged the box of envelopes inside, dropping it on the couch.

Out of habit, I turned up the heat. Without thinking, I poured some milk for the kitten. When I realized what I was doing, I muttered a curse. "You don't need another pet, Tony. Oscar's gone, and so is the hassle of feeding him."

I went into the bedroom, and to my surprise, the kitten had dutifully used the papers I had put down. After folding them and putting down fresh papers, I called the office and brought Marty up to date, after which I booted up the computer and went online.

I put in my request for arrest records on both Nelson Vanderweg and Nelson Villafono from Boulder, Colorado, then turned to the box of envelopes I'd hauled in from the evidence room.

Holderman must have had a penchant for privacy for only initials identified most of the individuals with whom he dealt. After perusing a couple of months of his calendar, I went back and jotted down each set of initials across the top of the page.

Every time the initials were mentioned, I listed the date beneath and the subject to the side. KN. Kim Nally. PJ, Perry Jacobs. ES, Eunice Seebell. Holderman wrote out his wife's name, Frances, along with two or three other names. Of the remaining five sets of initials, B, HW, AW, CCL, and BN, I figured out three; Al Waldron, Chu Cheng Lee, and the third, HW, I guessed to be Harper Weems. But, that puzzled me.

Thinking back, I remembered my interview with Weems. There was still something about the man that nagged at me, but I couldn't put my finger on it. Then I remembered. He had stated that he had no dealings with Holderman. The only words they ever exchanged were 'hi' and 'bye.' The initials on the desk pad plus the number of times they were inscribed on the pad seemed to indicate more than a simple greeting or brief farewell.

While I had figured out four of the five sets of initials, BN threw me until I found the same initials in a circled notation, DD, Elgin, on July 12, 1994. DD?

The jangling of the telephone interrupted me. It was Stewart to inform me he had found an apartment. "Six-fifty a month, but I'm sharing it with my friend."

"Sounds great, Stewart." I was pleased, but just a little surprised he had managed a job plus an apartment in the short time since he had arrived in Austin. I guess he knew what he was talking about when he told his father he had a job waiting. "What kind of job is it? You told me but I forgot."

He hesitated. "Delivery. A courier for Austin Expediters. We carry documents from business to business. Not much now, but I can move up as we expand."

"That's good. You call your Dad?"

"Sure did. Gave him my home address. You want it too?"

"Yeah."

He rattled off the address, which I recognized as the one I had driven past the night before.

I nodded. "Got it. Hey, what have you got on tonight? I thought I'd treat you to a big steak."

With just the right touch of disappointment in his voice, he replied, “I’d like to, Tony, but, truth is, I made other plans. You understand.”

I understood. If his friend was the soft voice I’d heard in the background the previous night, I would prefer her company myself. “No problem. Listen, anything you need, let me know. You hear? We’ll go out tomorrow or the next day, okay?”

“Gotcha, bro. Talk to you later.”

As soon as he hung up, I called Leroi with the good news, and if the truth were known, with a great deal of relief. Looking after a relative’s child would keep anyone’s nerves on edge.

Hanging up, I turned back to my computer, linking up to my white pages database. I searched for the initials DD in Elgin by inputting business, Elgin, Texas.

After a few minutes of searching the Ds, I stumbled across Dreamstreet Dancing Emporium. I grinned. Emporium? You bet, except in Texas emporiums are spelled h-o-n-k-y t-o-n-k-s.

And I remembered Chief Pachuca mentioning a topless bar in Elgin where Holderman picked up his wife, Frances Laurent Holderman.

At that moment, I would have bet my life savings, all $300, that this Dreamstreet Dancing Emporium, aka DD, was where George Holderman found his future wife.

Then I went back and listed each business he had noted on the pad, keeping a record on the number of times each was placed on the desk pad. Most were ordinary businesses; Hanks Barber Shop, Olympic Gym, the YMCA, a handful of restaurants, pharmacies, supermarkets—nothing out of the ordinary. Nothing unusual until, after about three or four years of desk pads, I suddenly noticed the single letter B beside Lupe’s Tacos on the February 2001 pad. I thumbed back to the earlier years. The name Lupe’s never appeared. Skimming forward, I found the B on the March and April 2001 desk pads. For the next few years, Lupe’s Tacos was mentioned once a month, each time marked with the B until June 2004.

Going back I rechecked all the pads back to '99, then forward to 2004. I was right the first time. There was no mention of Lupe's Tacos prior to 2001, and a reference to B only during the same time sequence.

Could that mean something? Who was B? I frowned at my notes. Or was I reaching too far? After all, Luby's Cafeteria was also mentioned once a month, same as Hanks Barber Shop, Willis Cadillac, and a dozen other businesses. And on occasion, some had initials beside them.

I shrugged off the question. If there was something significant regarding the initials, I'd learn it when I visited each of the businesses with a photograph of George Holderman.

That was one of the drawbacks of PI work. Usually it was days and days of tedious boredom and routine, shattered by unexpected moments of absolute panic.

I finished just before midnight. Exhausted, I skipped my shower and sprawled across the bed, telling myself that I might have wasted the entire evening. Every one of my fancy deductions might be wrong. Only time would tell.

Next morning, I turned my head and stared into the eyes of the tiny kitten curled on the pillow next to mine. I studied him a few moments. "You aren't staying Cat but I'm not throwing you out. I'm going to find you a home. A good home. Until then, don't sharpen your claws on my furniture, you hear?"

He started purring.

Rolling out of bed, I showered, shaved, and filled my insulated cup with coffee and nuked Cat a bowl of milk. I needed to pick up a bag of nuggets for him, a small bag because he wasn't going to be around very long, and I might as well pick up a litter box at the same time.

I checked my e-mail. Nothing from Boulder yet. I decided to wait for the report before calling the Ranchman's Motel.

I headed to the office, a folder full of notes at my side. The drizzle continued. The weather deteriorated throughout the day, but I had become so engrossed in reorganizing my notes, I failed to notice. I was amazed at Holderman's detail even though I didn't understand it completely.

KN was Kim Nally, and most of the notations concerning her were two and three years old, cryptic notes such as kn 2:30 coco or kn 7 es. Coco I interpreted as the Coconut Palms on 35 South or one of the four other nightspots with the same initials. Es could have been Embassy Suite or Eastern Steak House. For all I knew, it could have even been Emfingers Siding, but I couldn't see Holderman and Kim Nally meeting at Emfingers Siding at seven o'clock for a clandestine rendezvous among the vinyl sidings.

Of course, my entire premise was nothing more than a crapshoot, but it was the only crapshoot in town. For almost eighteen months, Kim Nally was a regular on Holderman's notepad. Abruptly, her name disappeared, after a June 8, 2003 note that read kn 100 bcp, dr h.

"Doctor H," I mumbled, "one o'clock." June 8, 2003, I discovered, fell on a Sunday. I stared out the window at the drizzle running down the panes. Why does anyone see a doctor on a Sunday? Obviously, an emergency. But, Holderman had it on his calendar. Nobody puts emergencies on a calendar.

Chapter Fifteen

On a hunch, I thumbed through the yellow pages. "Why am I not surprised," I muttered a few moments later, reading the ad. "Birth Control Planning, Dr. Evan J. Hodges." I shook my head. "The abortion Rita Viator had mentioned."

I gave myself a pat on the back. "Move over, Sherlock Holmes," I muttered, turning to the next set of initials.

ES, Eunice Seebell, the ex-secretary, who preceded Kim Nally as Holderman's mistress. Obviously, the superintendent collected mistresses like a Texas redneck collects gimme caps.

I considered her husband, Fred Seebell. He was an unlikely killer. If he had wanted to kill Holderman, why didn't he do it years back? "Maybe because he was waiting for just the right time," I muttered, answering my own question after reminding myself that he had ample time on the night of November 11. He didn't even have to sign in, only the teachers.

Around three, I left the office, deciding to run down BN at the Dreamstreet Dance Emporium in Elgin. See what he or she could tell me about the heartbroken Mrs. George Holderman.

* * *

The light rain continued, driving the winter chill deep into my bones. I shivered as I jumped out of my truck and headed for the padded door of the honky-tonk.

Inside, the club was dark and warm, filled with the sweet-sour smell of beer and whiskey. A couple of patrons perched on stools at the bar. The slowly flashing strobes bathed their faces first in red, then blue, then yellow, then green. I slid onto a stool and ordered a draft beer. When the bartender placed the icy mug in front of me, I handed him a business card and identified myself. "You the owner?"

A sallow-faced man with long black hair in his mid-thirties or so eyed me momentarily, then shook his head. "Nope. Bernie Neighbors." He wiped at the bar.

My eyes lit. BN. Bernie Neighbors. "You been working here long?"

He shrugged, continuing to wipe the bar. "Maybe."

"You know Frances Holderman? It was probably Laurent then."

"Maybe."

A wry grin ticked up on side of my lips. So that was how it was going to be. Like prying rocks out of concrete to get any information from him. So, I decided to take another angle. I'd lie. That was one talent in which I excelled. "Look, she's applied for a job with the company that retains me. I do background checks for them. That's what this is all about." I pulled out my small notebook and flipped through the pages. "According to her, she worked here up until about ninety-five."

The slender man paused in wiping the bar and looked up at me. "What'd you say her name was?"

"Frances Laurent. She was an exotic dancer. Headliner."

"Franny?" He snorted. "A headliner? Not quite."

My pulse quickened. "But, you knew her, huh?"

He glanced down at the two men at the bar, then leaned forward. "Not as Frances. Out here, she was Franny, and everyone knew Franny. Franny with the ready fanny, they called her. You know what I mean?" He gave me an obscene leer.

I nodded, and kept my mouth shut. He continued. "Nice looker. Great bod, but she was trouble. Bernie, he put up with her as long as he could. She brought a lot of customers in, but she sure caused a lot of trouble too."

"Oh?" I cocked an eyebrow.

"Yeah. Bernie's a decent sort, but after the cops came out two or three times because of her and threatened to close us down, Bernie canned her. She was trouble. Why, I remember once . . ." The grin vanished from his face. "Hey, you're in luck. Here's Bernie now."

I looked over my shoulder as a bowling ball of a man rolled across the floor toward us.

"You're early, Bernie."

Bernie paused and nodded to me before replying. "Had to drop my little girl off at the dentist. Wife's picking her up, so I thought I'd come on in."

The bartender introduced us and explained the purpose of my visit. He concluded with, "I was just telling him how you bounced Franny because of the trouble she was causing."

Bernie pursed his lips and absently smoothed at the few strands of hair combed across the top of his head. "What company did you say you were representing?"

I thought fast. "I didn't, but it's the Austin Christian Publishing House."

The bartender's eyes popped open. "Whoops." His cheeks colored. He glanced at the beer I had ordered. "Shouldn't that be a soft drink or milk, mister?"

"Just because I work for them doesn't mean I drink like them."

He laughed.

One of the patrons flagged the bartender. Bernie nodded at the man's retreating back. "Glenn's been with me almost fifteen years. He never liked Franny. Of course, she was pretty wild back then even if she was older than the other girls. Sometimes she'd get upset and come into my office for a good cry. I could tell then that she was basically an okay kid." He hesitated. "Well, maybe not a kid."

I did some fast calculations in my head. "She must've been about twenty-eight or thirty."

"Yeah." Bernie shook her head. "But she had the body of an eighteen-year-old. How she kept it, I don't know, but I was glad when she told me she was getting married. I didn't really know the guy, but the truth is, pal, a lot of these gals here can make the right guy a wonderful wife. I don't know what she'll be doing for your company, but I'm not afraid to tell you she'll be one good employee."

"She work here long, Bernie?"

He screwed up his face in concentration. "Yeah. Six or seven years. She never talked much about where she came from. I always had the feeling though she'd been through a rough marriage . . . or relationship like they call it nowadays. Like I said, she was a good kid. Most of my girls are."

"Your bartender said you fired her because she caused trouble."

Bernie shook his head briefly. "Yes and no. She couldn't help being a looker. If there was one fight over her, there was twenty. I would've kept paying the fines. She brought in twice what she cost me, but one day, she come in and told me she was getting married." He shrugged. "Just that simple."

I studied Bernie curiously. "You knew her husband?"

He nodded. "Not really. Oh, he was out here a lot for about a year before she left. I never talked to him. Kept to hisself. She never said much about what he did, but she did say he had a good job." Bernie frowned. "Things must be pretty tough on them now if she's got to work."

I made a couple of notes just to keep up my pretense. "Beats me. So, you think it was a good marriage, huh?"

"As far as she was concerned, Franny was thrilled." He paused. "Hey, if you see her, tell her if she needs anything, to get in touch with me. Okay?"

"Yeah." I nodded. He was a good man. "I will."

Heading home, I considered what I had learned. Regardless of her lifestyle, she appeared to love Holderman. Right then, I put her lower on the list of suspects.

Until later that night.

The drizzle plastering the windshield turned into a steady rain, the quintessential central Texas winter soaking that sent every living creature scurrying inside. On impulse, I pulled into a McDonald's for a Big Mac and family fries. Might as well clog the arteries with cholesterol and fat. On impulse, I also ordered a small burger for the kitten.

My apartment was warm and snug, a perfect refuge against the frigid weather outside. After cleaning the sauce off the kitten's burger and tearing the patty into small pieces for him, I wolfed down my own burger and fries.

Finally, I plopped down at my computer to type my notes for the day.

Just after 9:45, the phone rang.

I cradled it between my shoulder and ear so I could continue typing. "Hello."

"This the guy who was out at Dreamstreet today?" It was a woman's voice. The words were slurred.

"Yeah. Who's this?"

She ignored my question. "Hear you was nosing around, asking about Franny."

"Just doing my job. Who is this?"

"Look, I read about her in the paper last year, about someone bumping off her old man. If that's what you're really snooping into, then for the right amount of money, I can give you some choice information."

I rolled my eyes. "Yeah. I bet. Now, just what kind of information can you possibly give me?" My voice was heavy with sarcasm.

The woman dropped a bombshell in my lap. "She tried to hire me to find someone to kill her husband."

Chapter Sixteen

I froze. Everything about me froze. Time stood still. The clock on the kitchen wall stopped ticking. Even the kitten stopped purring.

Finally, I managed to swallow my heart, which had leaped into my throat, and with classic Tony Boudreaux poise, I stammered and stuttered, managing to choke out a gem of a question. "Who . . . Who is this?"

"Never mind. You interested?"

Was the fox interested in the chicken? "Yeah. Where are you?"

"Don't worry about that. Can you meet me tonight? About ten-thirty?"

I had regained my composure. "Sure. No problem."

"At Borgia's. On Sixth Street."

"How will I know you?"

"Don't worry. I'll know you."

I ran out into icy rain. Halfway to my truck, I realized I had left my jacket in the apartment. I ran back inside, grabbed it, and sprinted for my truck.

The rain stung my bare skin. Sleet. No one in his right mind should be out on the streets on a night like this, but I barged ahead in wild abandon, slowing only to pull into my ATM and withdraw a couple of hundred bucks.

Despite the weather, Sixth Street was hopping. Denizens from every culture of the underworld prowled the streets and slouched in bars half listening to the dissonant syncopation of ambitious, but musically challenged groups tearing through their gigs with strident, misplaced impetuosity.

Every parking spot was filled for two blocks around. I parked on a hill near the Omni Hotel, facing down just in case the sleet grew heavy. I could roll all the way down the hill to I-35.

Pulling my collar up around my neck and jamming my hands in the pockets of my jacket, I hurried along the cold, wet sidewalks, hunching close to the buildings in an effort to avoid some of the sleet. Suddenly, I rounded the corner into the glaring lights and deafening rap of Sixth Street. Borgia's, like the other bars and clubs, was busier than a hooker at the Democratic Convention.

Borgia's had no awning, so the sleet rat-tat-tatted against the front window. The water sheeting down the glass distorted the figures inside. I pushed through the door, pausing as a paroxysm of uncontrollable shivers racked my body. Slowly, they subsided as I eagerly soaked up the warmth of the establishment.

Like most clubs along Sixth Street, Borgia's interior was twenty feet wide and seventy-five deep. A bar, packed shoulder-to-shoulder with patrons, lined the first forty feet on one side. In the back corner of the room was a stage, on which four glassy-eyed musicians—a generous use of the word—in various states of undress banged on a piano, thrummed on a guitar, sawed on a bass fiddle, and screeched on a saxophone.

Round tables, each with four chairs, filled the remainder of the room. At first glance, I figured about eighty or ninety bodies, probably twice as many as the fire marshal would approve. I surveyed the room.

Next to the wall, near the front window, a pale hand waved. I made my way through the smoky room. A lone woman with half-shut eyes sat at the table, a cigarette dangling from her brightly painted lips. Her dark hair was straight and looked as if some time had passed since it had seen a good brushing. She wore a shapeless raincoat on which the water still beaded. There was a split in the plastic at the bend of her elbow. Overweight, she had reached that point where age is hard to guess. The puffy, blotched skin could belong to anyone from thirty-five to fifty-five. But, I wasn't about to guess, not aloud.

"You the one who called?" I stood behind a chair, staring down at her.

She squinted up at me, a faint sneer curling her lips. "I'll take a beer."

I hesitated, then shrugged. Why not? I got us each a draft beer and sat across the table from her. She slurped the beer and dragged the back of her hand across her lips. A dribble ran down her pointed chin and dripped on her raincoat.

Resting my elbows on the table, I leaned forward. "What's your name?"

She shook her head. "That ain't important."

I chuckled and patted my pocket. "If we make it worth your while, it is. For all I know, you could be figuring this was an easy string to pull. Take the money and run."

For several seconds, she stared at me, a mixture of greed and resentment flaring in her eyes. Greed won out. "Carrie Cochran. That's my stage name. I danced out at Dreamstreet with Franny."

"Go on." I leaned back and crossed my arms over my chest.

A wry grin played over her lips. "Like I said, I worked with Franny out there. We danced together when her hubby-to-be started hanging around. He was well off, she said, and he was pressuring her to marry him. She didn't love the guy, but like I said, he had money." Carrie shrugged. "I told her 'What the heck. Forget about love. Marry the guy. Money's better than love any day.' "

"Obviously she followed your advice."

She snorted. "Yeah. At least, they got married, and she left Dreamstreet. I hung around a couple more years, but finally . . ." Her voice grew soft and bitter. "Well, see for yourself. Time caught up with me, and I had to leave the runway. Those lecherous old men out there wanted to slobber over them thin little high school girls."

She sipped at her beer and continued. "Anyway, a few years later, Franny ran me down. I'm a hostess at the Marquee Club. Nice place. Good job. Good future."

I noted the frayed collar of her blouse. "That's nice," I replied. "So Franny, Mrs. Holderman, looked you up?"

"Yeah." She nodded emphatically. "She told me her old man had a big insurance policy on himself. Offered me a couple of thousand if I found someone who would whack him. Said she'd pay five thousand for the job." She drained her beer.

I slid my untouched beer across the table to her. She gave me a nod. "Anytime," I said. "Did you find someone?"

"Naw. Talked to a couple. But the money wasn't there for the risk, and Franny wouldn't go no higher."

I did some fast calculating. The time frame fit in neatly with Holderman's affairs with Eunice Seebell and later, Kim Nally. And that was about the time Holderman started going to Lupe's Tacos. Could it be he was meeting another woman out there? "Who were the guys you talked to?"

She looked at me in surprise. "Forget it. I ain't ready to lay my head down to sleep."

With a wry grin, I shook my head. "Come on, Carrie. Without some names, just how do you figure I can verify your story? I'm not handing any cash over just on your word. For all I know, this could be one big scam."

Her eyes flashed, but she remained silent. I could see the wheels turning in her head, slowly, but still turning. The anger gave way to indecision. "Look, Mr. Boudreaux, I could get bad hurt if I tell you too much."

I sensed a quiet desperation in her tone. I pulled out my wallet and slid her some bills. "Here's fifty. If I find out you're telling me the truth, there's another one-fifty. Okay?"

Her shoulders sagged. "I suppose I don't have any choice." Her eyes lit. "Hey, I could send you to—" She grimaced. "No, that won't work." She chewed on her lip in concentration. "Let me think a minute. Hey, maybe if you go see . . ."

She glanced past my shoulder and her heavily powdered face contorted with a grimace. "Oh, jeez," she muttered. She turned her head and gagged. "Gross."

I glanced over my shoulder to see what had distracted her. On the street beyond the front window, a slender black man, his features accented in harsh relief by the garish neon lights, was hunched over, puking his guts all over the sidewalk.

I froze, every muscle rigid. I blinked in disbelief. When I looked again, he had disappeared, but I would have sworn the guy was Stewart Wayne Thibodeaux, my cousin.

I jumped up, knocking my chair over.

Carrie exclaimed, "What—"

"I'll be back," I called over my shoulder.

Borgia's was jammed, the tables so close the backs of the chairs touched. I shot a glance at the window. He had disappeared. Muttering hurried excuses, I forced my way through, leaving a trail of acid-tongued women and cursing men behind.

A hand reached out to grab me, but I threw it off and lurched for the door, jerking it open and racing into the rain splattering on the sidewalk and soaking my legs. Several dark figures staggered down the sidewalk ahead of me, heads pulled down into their collars against the driving rain.

"Stewart!" I raced to the first cluster of three.

I grabbed the first one's arm. "Stewart?" I cocked my head to look into the man's face. A stranger looked back.

The second wino grabbed my arm. "Hey, buddy. How about a buck for some coffee?" The third one looked at me hopefully, his thin, bearded face reminding me of the pictures I had seen of those poor Jews caught up in the Holocaust of World War II.

All three were strangers. Hurriedly I pressed a couple of dollars into someone's grasping fingers and looked around frantically. The streets were empty.

I grimaced. Could I have been mistaken? The rain sheeting down the window distorted images like the House of Mirrors at the carnival. Maybe I had imagined it. Still, I would have sworn I had seen Stewart, but if I had, where in the blazes had he disappeared?

Ducking under a portico of a closed bar, I called his cell number. All I got was voice mail, so I told him to call me. After punching off, I glanced back up at Borgia's. I'd finish with Carrie as fast as I could and then swing by his place down on Festival Beach Street.

I headed back up the sidewalk, peering into darkened doorways, inside smoky bars. Nothing. At the corner, I made out three or four silhouettes stepping from the penumbra of light cast by the streetlamp and disappearing into the shadows of the alley.

"Stewart!" I yelled. "Wait!" I broke into a run, but by the time I reached the alley, the wraith-like shadows had vanished into the darkness.

I stood in the middle of the circle cast by the mercury streetlamp and stared into the night. The rain fell in torrents. I called out again. "Stewart! It's me! Tony!"

No answer except the thrumming of the rain on the pavement. Slowly, I made my way back to the bar, oblivious to the rain.

Chapter Seventeen

Carrie Cochran had vanished. Two couples sat at the table I had occupied less than five minutes earlier. I gestured to the bartender. "That woman I was with. You see her leave?"

His round face was slick with sweat. Brow furrowed, he studied me a moment. "Hey, you that guy who run out of here a few minutes ago, causing all the commotion?"

I shook my head. "I can explain. But not now. I got to find the woman I was with. Cochran. Carrie Cochran. You know her?"

He jabbed a sausage-like finger at me. The veins in his neck puffed out. "This is a high-class joint, buddy. We don't like no disturbances in here. Not unless you wanta get your rear kicked, you hear me?"

I held my temper. I wasn't going to find out a thing from this jerk except how fast he could come over the bar. I stepped back and held up my hand. "Sorry, bud. No problem."

He jerked his head toward the door. "Beat it."

I beat it, hugging the buildings as I made my way back up the hill to my pickup, cursing myself for leaving Carrie Cochran. She had been ready to give me a name.

The truck fired up. I flipped on the heat, making a mental note to look up Carrie Cochran out at the Marquee Club.

Within a couple of minutes, a blast of hot air filled the cab. I glanced in the direction Stewart had disappeared. What was he up to? Worry nagged at me.

Slowly, I drove the streets, hoping to spot Stewart, if indeed it had been Stewart I saw. On impulse, I headed for his place on Festival Beach Street.

Ahead, at the underpass of Seventh Street and I-10, red and blue strobes flashed, and the halogen beams of the police cruiser lit the wet street with a silver glow. Beyond the cruiser, a large sedan, both front doors open and the interior lights on, sat in the middle of the road.

Dark silhouettes scurried in and out of the headlights, hovering over an object lying in the street. I gripped the steering wheel tighter, fighting back the surge of fear squeezing off my breath. Could it be Stewart?

The sleet bouncing off his yellow poncho, an officer detoured traffic down the access road to the next underpass. I pulled over to the curb and parked.

A second cop stopped me as I approached the small crowd around the body sprawled in the street. "Sorry, buddy. Move on unless you got business here."

"Look, officer. I'm looking for my cousin. That might be him."

He shook his head. "Naw. It's an old broad."

I glanced over his shoulder just as one of the silhouettes moved, giving me a clear view of the inert body. It was Carrie Cochran. I closed my eyes. I muttered, "Is she dead?"

"Just about. Busted up good." He started to say more, but the investigating officer called him. He motioned me back to my pickup. "Go along now, buddy. We got enough traffic jamming up around here now."

I waited in my truck until the EMS team arrived. I noted the company, and then swung by the address Stewart had given me. His Pontiac was not in sight, and no one answered the phone. Worried sick, I headed home, crossing my fingers that Stewart was all right and that Carrie Cochran would live.

I stopped off to pick up a bag of kitten nuggets and a litterbox.

As soon as I closed the door behind me, I called Stewart again. To my surprise, he answered on the second ring. "Are you all right?" I asked.

He hesitated. "Something wrong, Tony?"

Now I was puzzled. The young man I had spotted in front of Borgia's looked like Stewart, but I must have been mistaken. "No. I thought I saw you earlier. I guess I was wrong."

"Hey, bro. I'm good. Just got in. Busy day."

"And you weren't down on Sixth Street?"

"Oh, yeah, yeah, man. I was. Got some bad food or something. Heaved my guts all over the sidewalk. I'm fine now."

Relieved that I hadn't been seeing things, I replied, "You sure you're okay?"

"Yeah, man. Plenty good. Job's good. I think I got me a good future here."

I shook my head wearily, grateful I didn't have a kid of my own. "When are we getting together?"

Stewart paused. "Let me give you a call, huh, Tony? I got plans the next couple of nights."

"Sure. No problem. Just stay in touch."

Next morning, the stormy weather had moved on to the east. The sky was clear, but the streets were still wet. I checked my e-mail. To my disappointment, Boulder, Colorado had no record of Nelson Vanderweg or Villafono. I read the rest of my mail, responded to a couple of letters from my old high school chat group, and then outlined my plans for the day, which included visiting with Jacobs and Nally at school before lunch, then Frances Holderman and Fred Seebell in the afternoon.

Before I left I called Travis County Hospital. Carrie Cochran was in ICU, critical condition.

Principal Howard Birnam asked me no questions. He showed me to the ARD meeting room and sent for Kim Nally and Perry Jacobs.

Jacobs had called in ill. I made a note to drop by his place, which would probably be a better spot for our talk than here at school.

While I waited for Kim Nally, I poured myself a cup of Seaport coffee and paused in front of Rita Viator's desk. She looked up, smiled, and nodded to the coffee. "Fresh and hot."

"And strong," I added.

Her smile grew wider at the compliment. "Next weekend, me and my husband, Walter, we go back to Lawtell to visit the old ones. 'Sides, the coffee, she is just about all gone. I bring back six cases."

I took another sip. Black, and rich, and fragrant. Even then, Rita had watered it down for the Texans' taste. Back in Church Point and Lawtell, folks served coffee in demitasse cups, and then only about three-quarters full.

The old folks believed the true test of good coffee was that it melted your dentures and shrunk your gums.

Rita scooted her chair a little closer to her desk. "Still interviewing, huh?" Curiosity oozed from her pores.

I lowered my voice. "Tell me, Rita. The abortion Kim Nally had. About when was that? You got any idea?"

She glanced around the office. No one seemed to be paying any attention to us. "Hard to say, but seems like a couple of years." She hesitated. "Why you ask?"

"Just curious." I shrugged. Two years corresponded with the June 8, 2003 date she had with Dr. Evan J. Hodges of the Birth Control Planning Clinic.

Kim Nally pushed through the door and nodded when she saw me. She wore a blue sweat top over blue shorts. Her legs were brown and lean with the firmness you'd expect from a physical education teacher. She spoke brightly. "Hi, Tony. I didn't expect to see you again so soon."

I held up the cup of coffee. "You know me and my coffee. This is the only place in three hundred miles to get a good cup."

She looked up at me expectantly. "What can I do for you?"

I gestured to the ARD room. "Just a couple of questions. Clarification really. Won't take five minutes."

She led the way and took a seat on the far side of the round table. I had discovered early in my so far unimpressive PI career that the best questions were usually the most direct ones. I began with a direct question. "Did Frances Holderman know about your abortion on June 8, 2003 at the Birth Control Planning Clinic?"

Chapter Eighteen

Her face turned to marble; her smile faded. She eyed me coldly. I added, "The doctor was Evan J. Hodges, Kim. I know all about it." I paused. "I've told no one about this. I know it's very personal, but I also know George Holderman set it up for you. Personally, knowing what I do about you, about your daughter, Alicia, and your dedication to her, I find it difficult to believe you would abort unless you were forced."

The icy expression on her face faded into a wry grin. "You think I killed George because he forced me to abort?"

"It's one dandy motive. I heard that Frances Holderman threatened a scandal if you didn't abort." I sipped the coffee casually. "Anything to that?"

Her eyes lit gleefully, as if she was harboring some deep, dark secret.

The amusement in her eyes unnerved me. "Something funny?"

She chuckled, arching an eyebrow in such a manner that instantly transformed her from a wide-eyed innocent into a hard-faced woman of the street. "It would be a dandy motive if it were true. But it isn't."

My jaw dropped open.

She narrowed her eyes. "Frances knew about the abortion. But she didn't threaten any scandal. In fact, she's the one who found Hodges. Abortions were his specialty. She knew him from her old days. I never asked, but I imagine she used him once or twice herself." The brown-haired PE teacher gestured at me. "Close your mouth. You'll catch flies."

"Huh?" I closed my mouth. The candor of her sordid admissions had stunned me. Regardless of the feminist movements of the seventies and eighties pushing into various bastions of masculinity, I was still of the school that believed in mother and home and apple pie.

"I wanted the abortion." She leaned forward, her eyes blazing. "You have any idea how expensive it is for a single mother to rear an autistic child?" Without giving me time to reply, which I couldn't have anyway, she said, "You do it because you love them. You do everything for them. The cold, hard truth is I didn't have time for another." She shrugged. "So I aborted." The fire in her eyes grew as cold as ice, daring judgment.

"What about Holderman?"

"What do you mean?"

"The abortion. He want it?"

A faint sneer twisted her lips. "Poor George. He wanted whatever Frances wanted."

I blinked in surprise. "What?"

"Yeah. Whatever Frances wanted, George did."

Suddenly I had the picture. "So you're saying that when you learned you were pregnant, you went to Frances Holderman? She set up the abortion, and George was simply the wheel man."

"No." She shook her head. "Nothing like that. When Frances found out about me and George, she pitched a fit. I had just discovered I was pregnant, and I didn't need the additional hassle of a betrayed wife. I broke it off with George, and at the same time I told him I wanted the abortion. He said he'd find someone. So, he went to the most logical source for a doctor who performed abortions, his own wife."

I hesitated. Something didn't make sense. "You mean, despite the fact she was upset about you and George, she still helped you out?"

She arched an eyebrow. "Hey, Tony, it wasn't as if she were a pristine virgin or anything like that. Sure, she was upset, but she knew he was fooling around. He was always fooling around. It upset her when she found out I was the one he was fooling around with. But she cooled off in a hurry when she realized if I didn't abort, I would demand child support money. She knew George's history. In fact, she'd played the game before. That's how she got him." Her voice dropped to a lower timbre. "Before me, he slept with Eunice Seebell. According to Frances, he'd had a couple of affairs earlier, even before he came to Safford ISD. Naturally, Frances was angry when she found out about me, but by then, she was used to his philandering."

I glanced at my notepad. "You split the sheets in 2003. Who came afterward? I mean, after you?"

She shrugged. "I think Frances stopped George." She chuckled at a secret joke, then winked at me. "The truth is, I think she swore to do a little clipping if he didn't behave. You know, the Lorena Bobbitt thing."

When I first met Kim Nally, she had reminded me of a Sunday School teacher, but now I knew my innocent little Sunday School teacher was in truth not an innocent Sunday School teacher after all.

She narrowed her eyes. "Look, Tony. I don't care what you or anyone thinks about me. My personal life is mine." Her eyes grew soft. "My child wants for nothing. She never will. Maybe one day, she can go out on her own, in a small sort of way." A wicked gleam grew in her dark eyes. "In the meantime, when I feel the itch, I'll find somebody to scratch it."

She stared at me defiantly.

I stared back at her. I grinned. A slow smile played over her lips in return. "Tell me one more thing, Kim."

She stiffened. I sensed her growing antagonism. "No. Not

about you." She relaxed visibly, and I continued. "I was going over Holderman's appointments, I discovered seven sets of initials, yours included. Now, I think I know what relationship most of them had with Holderman, but there is one set that puzzles me. HW. The only school person I know with those initials is Harper Weems." I didn't tell her that something had been nagging at me about Weems.

She nodded. "So?"

"So, do you know if Weems and Holderman had any business deals together?"

"Not that I know of. I didn't think they had anything to do with each other outside of school, but I could be wrong."

I made a few notes in my notepad. "Weems been teaching here long?"

Her forehead wrinkled in a faint frown. "I've been here nine years. Harp was here when I came. I think he's been here fifteen years or so."

An idea popped into my head. "He always been in the wheelchair?"

"He was when I got here. Motorcycle wreck. I don't know how long ago. Paralyzed from the waist down. Can't move a muscle, but I think I told you that before."

"But, didn't he have some kind of accident just a few years ago? Seems like he mentioned it to me."

"Yeah. He was out for a couple of years or so. Wrecked his van on the way to visit his brother in Colorado. Some kind of amnesia, but he's fine now." She hesitated. A curious grin played over her tanned face. "Surely, you don't suspect Harp, do you?" When I didn't reply immediately, she exclaimed, "You do. You think Harp might have killed George." Her tone was incredulous.

"Well"—I shrugged—"stranger things have happened."

She giggled. "Harp wouldn't hurt a fly. Besides, Mr. PI," she said with a touch of amused sarcasm in her tone, "how would he get upstairs? Don't forget. We're in the old wing. And it was built forty years before all the fancy handicapped stuff became mandatory. No elevators. Not even a handicapped men's room. What do you think he might have done, walked on his hands upstairs and then back down?"

That was it. That was what had been nagging at me about Weems. His hands. That was it. His hands were soft. They should have been callused from fifteen years of pushing a wheelchair.

Nally spoke up again. "You can't be serious about Harp."

I ducked my head, then looked up at her. "It would have been a good trick, wouldn't it?" But that was exactly what I was now thinking. Of course, I hadn't figured out just how Harp could have slipped up on Holderman with the ball bat. Unless he wasn't paralyzed. But if he wasn't, then what kind of game was he playing?

She laughed. "Yeah. It would have been a good trick."

"So," I added, shifting the subject, "who do you think killed him?"

She shrugged. "Beats me. I didn't, and I don't think Perry Jacobs did either. And I know Harp couldn't."

"No ideas at all?"

She grew thoughtful. "I've studied it. I don't see how anyone could have slipped in there, killed George, then got away without someone spotting them. You've talked to everyone who went into that wing, haven't you?"

"What about someone slipping out the front door of the lobby, cutting across the quadrangle to the side door of the old wing?"

Kim arched an eyebrow. "Frances?"

She was quick. I grinned. "Or Fred Seebell."

She shrugged. "The band uses the quadrangle for practice. That was football season, and during that time, they use the quadrangle every night. The band director, Chase Sherman, might have spotted someone. He always videos band practice."

A surge of excitement coursed through my veins. "Chase Sherman, you say." I jotted the name.

"Yeah. Maybe he can help."

Chapter Nineteen

Dropping by the band hall, I visited with Chase Sherman. As he slipped the video of November 11, 2004 in the VCR, he explained, "We video all our practices from three different angles. If anyone was out there, they'll be on video."

For two hours, I reviewed each of the three angles from 8:40 to 9:45. Not a single soul cut across the quadrangle to the side doors.

I grimaced. The videos blew the heck out of my little theory that either Fred Seebell or Frances Holderman could have slipped away from the reception and through the side door unobserved. And their names were not on the list kept by the hall monitors. Consequently, if they couldn't get to Holderman, they couldn't kill him.

As I headed back to my pickup, I reprised my theories about the others. Tentatively, I eliminated Kim Nally as a suspect, pending Frances Holderman's verification of Nally's version of her abortion.

Although I had concocted a possible scenario involving Harper Weems, I found it difficult to believe he was the killer. I did want to completely eliminate him from any suspicion, and the easiest way was to find out if he could walk or not.

Remembering the two flats on my previous visit, I checked the tires before I moved my pickup. Whoever was playing tricks was serious this time. They had placed a roofing nail under each of the four tires. I removed them and dropped them in my pocket.

I studied the building before me, wondering if my trickster was standing at a window watching, and laughing.

I headed for the Safford ISD administration building. From the assistant superintendent of personnel, I learned the identity of Weems' primary care doctor, J. Marion Jeffcoat.

At three o'clock, I finally managed to see Dr. J. Marion Jeffcoat, who proved grudgingly accommodating, not so much because of my charm, personality, and devastating good looks, but because of a telephone call from Billy Vanbiber, Chief of Police, Safford, Texas, a call I had requested the chief make.

Jeffcoat was angry when the nurse showed me into his office. "I don't have much time, Mr. Boudreaux, so if you'll tell me what you want, I'll answer as quickly as I can." His words were hard and clipped.

"Harper Weems, Doctor. The accident that paralyzed him. That's all I'm looking for."

He nodded to the nurse. She disappeared, leaving us alone in the office. The tension was palpable. I tried to be pleasant. "Nice place you have here, Doc."

His eyes were wide-set and icy green. "Harp in trouble?"

"Nope. Just a description of the injury that paralyzed him."

The nurse re-entered and handed the doctor a folder.

He jerked the file open and began reading in a frustrated monotone. "Patient severed his spinal cord at L Four and Five in a motorcycle accident fourteen years ago. Post-operatively, he underwent two years of intensive therapy, was released, confined to a wheelchair, and eventually the patient resumed his fulltime teaching position."

I saw a manila envelope in the folder. "Those the x-rays?"

With a disgusted grunt, Dr. Jeffcoat looked around at me. "I suppose you want to see them."

His curt response got under my skin. "Doc, I want to see everything you have. If not here, then down at the station." I was bluffing, and I hoped he didn't call my hand.

He snapped a dozen x-rays on the viewing screen. "Here"—he said, pointing to the first—"is the initial injury." He went on to point out the same spot on five more x-rays. "And these last two," he added, "were shot just three months ago." He looked at me. "You have any kind of medical background?"

"Not a bit, Doc. All I need is for you to show me on these x-rays what keeps him from walking."

He indicated the spinal column, which looked like a series of tiny white spools stacked on top of each other. He pointed to a gray cord. "This is the spinal cord. It runs down the lumbar vertebrae."

"Lumbar vertebrae?"

He glanced at me, then turned back to the x-ray, shaking his head wearily. "The backbone you call it." He indicated the backbone several inches above the tailbone. "Right here, between the fourth and fifth lumbar vertebrae, the spinal cord is severed." He indicated the gray cord. "If you look closely, you'll see the separation."

I squinted at the x-ray. I pointed to a collection of vague light and dark images. "Right here?"

"Yes."

With a nod, I stepped back.

"I know you aren't sure just what you're looking at here, Mr. Boudreaux, but take my word. Once the spinal cord is severed, an individual loses all hope of bipedal ambulation."

"Bipedal ambulation?" I frowned at him.

"Walking. This is Harper Weems' condition, and Harper Weems will never walk again."

"Thanks, Doc. One more question, and I'm out of here. Was this the accident where he suffered from amnesia?"

"No." He glanced down at Weems' records. "That was in 2000 or 2001. I didn't treat him. He was up in Colorado visiting his twin brother. His brother nursed him through that period." He glanced at the folder, then indicated the last two x-rays on the viewing glass. "But, like I said, those two were made three months ago."

"Thanks, Doc." I turned to leave, then hesitated. "You said that last accident was in Colorado?"

"Yes. Denver." He gave me a curious look. "Why?"

I shrugged. "Nothing. Just idle curiosity, Doc. That's all." I was curious to know why Weems had left out the fact that his brother was his twin. Were they identical or fraternal? That might place an interesting skew on the investigation.

Chapter Twenty

The winter sun had dropped behind the hills to the west, and the temperature began to fall. I climbed in my Silverado, making a note to check on Harper Weems' brother and inquire into the relationship between Harp and Holderman.

Next stop, Perry Jacobs. I pulled out my notepad and looked up his address. Shifting my pickup into gear, I headed for 476 Canyon Road.

I have never ceased to be amazed at the creativity land developers use in naming streets. There was no creek near Brown Creek Trail, nor a terrace within miles of Jason Terrace Drive, and Canyon Road was a straight street down the middle of the flattest land around.

Jacobs' house was a single garage dwelling with vinyl siding in a neighborhood of single garage, vinyl-sided homes. About what you would expect a schoolteacher could afford. Some were L-shaped, some T-shaped, some I-shaped. Every other house was flip-flopped in a futile effort to suggest diversity among the floor plans.

The neighborhood was well-kept, probably older people whose hobbies were gardening and mowing the yard. I pulled into the driveway of number 476. I wasn't sure what to expect.

Jacobs had been belligerent, almost pugnacious at our last meeting.

Jacobs answered the door, his sallow face and the dark rings around his eyes reminding me of a Halloween mask. "Stinking flu," he muttered, staring listlessly at me through the screen door.

The warmth of the house hit me, a heavy mixture of Vicks, Nyquil, and whiskey. "I can come back."

He shrugged. "Wife works the evening shift. Might as well come on in. Unless you're afraid you'll get the flu." He pushed the screen open. The dark bags under his eyes hung like sagging hammocks. A thin gray beard covered his flopping jowls. "I figured we'd covered everything the other day." His remark was anything but belligerent.

I followed him into a living room lit by three lamps and a TV. "Almost. I only have a couple of points to clear up."

He plopped in a worn leather recliner and turned down the volume on the TV. The end table next to the recliner was covered with various medications, crumpled paper tissues, and a bottle of cheap whiskey. The room smelled of the flu. I sat across the room from him, perching on the edge of a floral couch with threadbare cushions, operating on the premise that the less I came in physical contact with anything in the house, the less chance I had of contracting the flu.

Jacobs blew his nose and popped a couple of pills, washing them down with a gulp of whiskey. He leaned back. "Shoot."

I shot.

"How much money did you lose on the investment scheme Holderman recommended?"

He simply stared at me, his dull eyes unseeing. After several moments, he released a long sigh. "So you found out about that, huh?"

"Yeah. How did you figure on keeping something like this quiet? You sell off the family home and put every cent you have into a land deal that Holderman recommended. He bails out.

The deal falls though. You lose everything." I shook my head. "Truth is, Jacobs. If I were the District Attorney, you'd be booked so fast, your head would spin."

I hesitated, waiting for his reaction. He remained motionless.

His silence puzzled me. "What about your contract? You make all that up?"

After a moment, he shook himself from his lethargy and focused on me. He had the eyes of a beaten man. "No. I did threaten George. He came back with the threat to deny me a contract. His appraisals were the means he planned to use to get rid of me."

"And?"

He dropped his head and stared at his battered hands folded in his lap. "After a few months when I saw he was serious, I begged him not to." Tears filled his eyes. "I actually begged that no good . . . well, I begged him for my job. Begged, and that's when he told me we'd talk more about it after the PTA meeting." He paused. His tone pleaded for me to understand. "Why would I kill him when there was a chance he was going to let me keep my job? Huh? You understand what I'm saying?"

I stared into the pleading eyes of a frightened man. "From what I learned, Holderman got out of the scheme about a year before it folded. He tried to talk you into getting out. Is that right?"

Slowly, Perry Jacobs nodded. "Yeah." He drew a deep breath. "The truth is, I just got greedy. I saw him step out with a little over a half-million profit. I figured I could do the same, so I hung in there."

"Half million?" I thumbed through my notes. "According to Waldron, Holderman didn't make any kind of profit. He claimed that Holderman lost over half his initial investment."

Jacobs stared at me in disbelief. "How do you know that?"

"I told you. Waldron. The real estate agent." I jabbed at the notebook with my finger.

"Waldron." He said the word as if he was massaging it in

wonder. A quizzical frown knit his forehead. "Waldron said that, huh?"

"Yeah."

"I don't understand."

"What? What don't you understand?"

"You don't suppose," he said, speaking more to himself than me. "No." His eyes took on a faraway look.

"Suppose what? Come on, Jacobs. Suppose what?"

Suddenly, he came back to the present. "Huh? Oh, oh." He chuckled. "Sorry. I was just thinking. George had an ego. A big ego. You know, the braggard could have done just that."

"Just what?" I was growing impatient.

He leaned forward. "I didn't think about him losing money. The way he talked, I figured he'd come out ahead, but now it makes sense. Understand, I'm not saying this is what happened, but he was the kind of man who hated to admit he lost out on anything. When he first approached me about the deal with Lee, I told him he was a sucker for taking that kind of risk. Now, I know he made a profit at first. So maybe, when his investment began slipping away, he bailed out, and deliberately kept the truth from me so I wouldn't rub it in."

I understood his point, convoluted though it was. "Maybe so."

Jacobs gave a short laugh. "Oh, no question. That's the kind of thing George Holderman would do."

"Still, you're the only one besides Kim Nally who had the opportunity and motive to kill Holderman."

His eyes narrowed. His face grew hard, then relaxed. He leaned back and reached for the nose spray. After dosing both nostrils, he said, "I see where you're coming from. I'd probably see it the same way. All I can tell you is that I didn't kill him."

Regardless of how bad it looked for Perry Jacobs, I didn't believe he was the killer. Still, I couldn't prove he wasn't. There was opportunity and motive, one heck of a motive.

* * *

My breath caught in my throat, and I jerked to a halt when I reached my pickup. I don't know what infuriated me most, the bullet hole in the windshield on the passenger's side, or the note under the windshield that read: NEXT TIME YOU'LL BE BEHIND THE WINDSHIELD.

Crumpling the note in my fist, I looked up and down the street. There was no trace of activity. Muttering a curse, I jammed the note in my pocket and yanked the door open. The slug had passed through the rear window also.

For several minutes, I sat motionless behind the wheel, staring out the window. I tried to shift my focus from the anger boiling in my blood back to the case at hand. I went back over my list of suspects.

For all practical purposes, I hadn't proven anyone guilty, nor had I eliminated anyone completely from suspicion. Harper Weems was a long shot, and I was halfway kicking my own tail for bothering with him, but what if his brother was an identical twin? What if he and his brother had switched places that night? But, why? What motive could Weems have had?

I figured I was pushing the envelope on Weems, but sometimes you pushed, and it paid off. Other times . . . well, you pushed and nothing happened.

Seebell and Holderman had motive, but to reach George Holderman, they would have had to sprout wings. And then there was Perry Jacobs and Kim Nally, both of whom had motive and opportunity. On the other hand, if Frances Holderman supported the PE teacher's allegations concerning the abortion, that would take Nally's motive off the table.

I shook my head. "You're batting a zero, Boudreaux. You got one dead man, six suspects, and you still don't have a glimmer as to who whacked Holderman. Or why."

Chapter Twenty-one

On the drive out to visit Frances Holderman, I couldn't help but think about Stewart. From what he said, it appeared he was doing just fine. Still, a niggling little worry nagged at me. I decided to see what I could find out about Austin Expediters. Maybe that would make me feel better.

I whistled when I pulled through the brick gates at the entrance to Brentwood Hills, an upscale community spreading over the rolling hills looking out over Lake Travis west of Austin. Sprawling one and two-story structures were surrounded by manicured lawns accented by trimmed greenery that edged the broad brick drives.

I knew public school superintendents made good money, but not this good. He must have been moonlighting or playing the Louisiana slots for there was no way a $125,000 income could purchase anything out here except maybe a garden hothouse, and then on a ten-year mortgage.

I thought back over my notes concerning Frances Holderman, maiden name Laurent. Motive, a betrayed woman with eight million bucks at stake. According to neighbors, more than once she had threatened her husband for his philandering.

The details of their marital battles were no secret. And, like icing on a cake, she had solicited a hit man for her husband.

To my surprise, Frances Holderman answered the door. She wore a sheer negligee, gossamer white. Her eyes were bright, her face flushed, her voice a little too loud. Even my meager powers of deduction had no trouble surmising she was drunk even if she hadn't answered the door with a cocktail in her hand.

"Ah. Mr. . . ."—she snapped her fingers—"oh, yes, Mr. Boudreaux." She arched an eyebrow.

I hesitated, reluctant to proceed since she was obviously inebriated. "I know it's late, Mrs. Holderman. I can come back if this is a bad time."

She laughed. "Oh, no. No time is a bad time, Mr. Boudreaux." She hesitated, knit her brows in puzzlement. "Or maybe I should say no time is a good time." With an indifferent shrug, she stepped back and opened the door wide. "Oh, well. No matter. Please, come in. Join me in the study." Without waiting for a reply, she turned on her heel and moved unsteadily across the foyer, leaving me standing.

I shrugged. *Carpe diem!*

Sometimes, you seize the moment. I seized it, closed the door and followed her, noting the slight stagger in her walk.

The study was straight out of a Hollywood movie set, lush carpet, bookcases inset in the walnut-paneled walls, highly polished tables about the room, leather chairs and couches, and a brightly burning fire in the hearth. She flicked a limp hand toward a credenza against one wall. "Fix yourself a drink." She plopped down on one end of the couch and drew her legs up under her. "Ice in the bucket."

I poured a glass of water and dropped a couple of cubes of ice in it. "Nice place," I said, sitting in a chair opposite her and nodding to the study.

She smiled sadly. "Lonesome without George here." She

gave a long sigh followed by a bitter laugh. "It was lonesome with George here." Leaning her head back on the couch, she stared at the ceiling. "I thought it would get easier with time, but it hasn't."

One thing I had to say for her, she sounded sincere, but that didn't fit with what Carrie Cochran had told me. "If you don't mind, Mrs. Holderman. I've got a couple of questions that I need answers for."

She looked me straight in the eye. "That's why I'm paying your company, Mr. Boudreaux. I expect results."

"Results, huh?"

"Yes."

I hit her squarely between the eyes with my next question. "Is that why you tried to find a hit man for your husband?"

A heavy silence filled the study. The cocktail glass fell from her suddenly lifeless fingers. It bounced on the carpet and spilled onto the shag. She didn't move. For a moment, I thought my question might have brought on a coronary or precipitated a stroke. Then she blinked her eyes.

I continued. "I heard you started looking when you learned that your husband was having an affair with Kim Nally."

She caught her breath. Her eyes flashed fire. "I . . . I resent the implication. Who . . . where did you hear that?"

I sipped my water and leaned back in the chair, crossing one leg over the other. I replied in a soft, unthreatening tone. "Look, Mrs. Holderman. I know your background, the dancing at Dreamstreet, the customers, the problems. I know about your husband's affairs. Now none of this confirms you as your husband's killer. To be honest, I don't think you are, but until I can find some answers and clear up some questions, you're still a primary suspect. As far as I know, you could have hired someone to hide in the closet in Jacobs' room. Waiting until your husband came in."

The fire faded from her eyes. "But . . . I hired you to find the killer. Why would I do that if I was responsible?"

I laughed. She frowned at the skepticism in my laughter. "Could be you thought it a clever move for that very reason. You could have figured the cops wouldn't suspect you if you hired someone to find the killer." I took another drink. "The oldest trick in the world. Misdirection." I paused to let the words sink in. "So, tell me about your little plot."

Indecision scribbled a frown across her face. Should she deny, deny, deny, or tell the truth? She forced a weak smile. "I could use another drink."

"No problem." I rose and crossed the room to the credenza. I reached for the ice.

"Just straight."

I grinned to myself and poured her a tumbler of Jim Beam Black Label. One thing about her, she bought good bourbon.

"Here you go." I handed her the glass and sat back down in my chair.

She downed half the tumbler, shivered, then stared at me defiantly. "I knew George could never be faithful. He cheated on his second wife with me, so why should I expect him to be true to me?"

She paused, took another drink, and continued. "He was okay for the first couple years, then that Seebell woman, that shrewish little secretary came along, and next that PE teacher. At first, I was stunned, then I got mad."

"That's when you started looking for someone, huh?"

"Yes." She paused, studying me as if she were trying to read my mind. "Who told you, Carrie Cochran?"

"Carrie who?"

A faint sneer twisted one side of her lips. "Yeah. It had to be Carrie. She was the only one I went to. Offered her two thousand to find someone. I told her I'd pay five for the job, but she didn't find anyone. By then, I'd cooled off and changed my mind." Taking a deep breath, she lifted her hand and made a sweeping gesture to the study. "After all," she said with heavy sarcasm, "where is someone like me going to find another place like this?"

I arched an eyebrow. That question, I couldn't argue.

She laughed, but I could hear the edge of bitterness in it.

I changed the direction of the interview. "You do have a nice place here."

"Thanks." She sipped her bourbon.

"Did George have some other income?"

She frowned.

I explained. "It's hard to figure this kind of place on a superintendent's salary." I looked around the richly appointed study. "Place like this, I'd figure a couple of million."

She remained silent a moment, then shrugged. "I can't really say. George handles . . . I mean, handled all the bills and legal stuff. Our attorney does it now. George said it was paid for. He showed me the title before he put it in the safety deposit box."

I arched my eyebrows. "Well, it is a fine place, Mrs. Holderman. A fine place."

"Thank you."

In the next breath, I changed the subject. "Nally told me she came to you for the abortion."

Whatever reaction I had expected from her, I didn't get. Holderman closed her eyes and shook her head dreamily. "Can you believe it? She sent George to me for a name . . . you know, a doctor who can keep his mouth shut."

"So you gave her Hodges' name, Dr. Evan J. Hodges?"

A wry smile curled her lips. She leaned forward, propping her elbow on the arm of the couch. "You know something funny. I liked her guts. Still do. Hey, what did she do that I haven't done, or a million women like us? Yeah, I sent her to Hodges. A bunch of us had used him. He was reasonable, and he kept his mouth shut. I'd known . . ."

I nodded slowly. She began to ramble now as the whiskey dulled her thinking. As far as I was concerned, her admission had eliminated Kim Nally from suspicion. The PE teacher had told the truth. While she had the opportunity, I could see no motive, no reason for her to murder George Holderman.

"What about Harper Weems? Your husband ever mention him? Business dealings, school affairs, anything of that sort?"

She mulled my question a moment. "No. I know Mr. Weems. The cripple, right?"

I nodded. She continued. "But, to be honest, I never heard George mention his name. Not once."

Disappointed, I folded my notepad back into my pocket, finished off my drink, and rose. "Thanks, Mrs. Holderman."

She tried to rise, but her legs refused to support her. With a silly grin, she leaned back on the couch. "You can show yourself out, okay?"

"Yeah. Okay."

Chapter Twenty-two

I reached my apartment just after nine. Calling my insurance agent, I made an appointment to have my truck windows replaced the next day. Then I called Fred Seebell, arranging an interview for nine o'clock the next morning at his business, the Congress Avenue Pharmacy.

To be honest, I figured I was wasting my time. Both the list compiled by the hall monitors and the video shot by Chase Sherman, the band director, exonerated Seebell, but until I interviewed him, my investigation was not complete. I grumbled. "The only way he could have reached Holderman was to have made himself invisible or grown wings."

Next, taking care to block my call with a *67, I rang the Ranchman's Motel in Amarillo, uncertain as to how I could pry information about Vanderweg aka Villafono from the staff of the motel. The night clerk, whom I guessed to be an older man by the palsy in his voice, answered. Putting on my best detective voice, I took the part of a lieutenant for the Houston Police Department. "We're trying to run down the whereabouts of Nelson Villafono. He stayed with you a few weeks back."

"Sorry. The name doesn't ring a bell," the old man replied,

his tone indifferent. I had the feeling I'd interrupted his favorite TV program.

"I'd appreciate if you'd check your records, sir. You see, we suspect him of being part of a scam that has hit several cities in the state by taking advantage of our elderly citizens. Promises of new roofs or patching driveways. This guy gets the money up front for materials, then vanishes. You'd be doing us a big favor if you can come up with some information about him." I crossed my fingers, hoping I'd guessed right about the clerk.

His reaction was more than I hoped. "Why, that dirty . . . there was a bunch of them what come through here a few years back, but I didn't fall for it."

I couldn't resist grinning. He probably leaped at their offer like a ten-pound bass at a June bug and got himself hooked tight. "Can you see if he was there?"

"You bet. Hold on."

He left me listening to Willie Nelson music. When he came back, he had what I'd been hoping for. "Yeah. He was here the first week in October. I remember him because he checked in driving a beat-up Olds and left in a black Mercedes. I wondered where he got the money. Now I know."

"What home address did he give when he registered?"

"Huh?"

"Home address. When he registered. What home address did he give?"

"Oh, okay. Let's see. "Phoenix. Explorer Apartments on Silverado Street, 67203 Silverado."

"How long did he stay with you?"

"I don't know. Let's see." I heard him counting under his breath. "About five weeks or so."

I thanked the old man and hung up. Five weeks. He must have remained around for some time after buying the Mercedes. Why?

It was almost ten, but if I remembered my time zones right, it was nine in Phoenix. I called Explorer Apartments.

The apartment manager hesitated when I asked about Nelson

Villafono. "You got the wrong name. I don't know no Villafono, but I sure know Nelson Vanderweg."

Bingo. "Maybe it is Vanderweg," I replied.

He almost yelled. "You know where that guy is? He left here owing a month's rent plus damages to his place. He even threatened me with a lamp. You a friend of his?"

I gave him the same story I gave the night clerk. "Now, one question, Mr. . . . I'm sorry, what was your name?"

He replied without hesitation. "Carey. Wylie Carey."

"Well, Mr. Carey. Didn't you do some kind of background check on him before leasing the apartment?"

"Yeah. We don't let trash in our place here. He didn't have any criminal record in Arizona. I've got the report in my file."

I held back a shout of joy. I couldn't believe my luck. In a controlled voice, I asked, "How long was he there?"

"Couple months."

"Would you mind taking a look at his report and see if there's any previous addresses. We're anxious to get our hands on this guy."

Carey grunted. "Sure. Hold on." I could hear drawers opening and closing, then the riffling of paper.

"Okay. Here we are. Eugene, Oregon. That where he says his home was."

"Any address, telephone number."

"Naw. His parents, Willam W. Morrison. Stepdad, I guess."

I thanked him, promised to stay in touch, and hung up. Immediately, I dialed information in Eugene, Oregon. No William Morrison, nor Bill, nor WW, nor any combination.

Then a wild idea hit me.

I called the motel in Pampa again. The old man answered, his voice drugged with sleep. I apologized. "I need one more piece of information. You said Villafono registered driving an Oldsmobile?"

"So?"

"Did you get the license?"

"We always take down the license."

"Can I have it?"

Moments later, I jotted it down. Arizona. I grinned. Finally, a break.

Danny O'Banion is a local entrepreneur with his fingers and toes in every pot in Travis County. Actually, he's Austin's resident mobster. Of course, no one calls him that to his face, but the best I can figure he's about half a step below the family concierge. Perhaps, a better explanation is that he's the concierge for the concierges, a sort of liaison between those at the top and the soldiers at the bottom.

But whatever explanation you can give for Danny O'Banion, he has influence over a large portion of Texas, and numerous friends in Louisiana who owe him big favors.

Danny and I had a history. Back in the eleventh grade, we scrambled through a few scrapes together. Then Danny left school before his senior year. Naturally, we drifted apart, but those months during our junior year bonded us. I ran into him at one of the annual football games between my alma mater UT and Oklahoma up in Dallas one year. We hit each other on the shoulder, lied a little, sipped from his silver flask a lot, and then went our separate ways.

A few years earlier, I had saved his bosses a couple of suitcases of heavy coin. In doing so, I picked up a lead slug but gained their gratitude. I always figured I got the best of that swap. So, now, I hoped Danny might be willing to give me a hand.

Not only did he agree to find every scrap of information and dirt he could on Nelson Vanderweg or Villafono, but he insisted on taking me to dinner the next night. "At the County Line," he said. "I've been hungry for barbecue and cold beer."

Chapter Twenty-three

Congress Avenue Pharmacy remained open twenty-four hours a day. The weather had moderated, but the wind was still from the north, taking a break, gathering its strength to usher in the next front.

Fred Seebell was medium height, slender with short hair neatly coiffed. In fact, he looked like a New York stockbroker in a white lab jacket behind the counter.

After I introduced myself, he nodded to his assistant. "I'll be back in my office, Cole."

Without a word, he led me down a narrow hall and into a cramped but neat office. He gestured to a chair as he slipped into the wood swivel chair behind his desk. "Please, have a seat, Mr. Boudreaux."

Seebell must've been a no-nonsense businessman for he came straight to the point. "Personally, I'm glad someone killed George Holderman. I'll probably burn in Hades for saying so, but it's the truth." He leaned forward, his eyes serious. "We are religious people, Mr. Boudreaux, my wife and I. And I know what it means to my soul to hold such hatred in my heart. I've tried to take it out, but I can't. And I won't lie about it. I thought about killing him after he seduced my wife and led her along for so many months. I even had the opportunity once or twice, but, well . . ." His brow furrowed, and he stared down at his hands. "I just didn't have the guts to do it.

"That lecherous spawn of Satan almost ruined my life, but thank the Lord, Eunice and I have a wonderful preacher. He worked hard with us, and now, we've forgiven each other, and our lives are good."

I've never been too surprised at the way some people respond to questions. Some skirt the question like Al Waldron, the realtor. Others, like Seebell or Kim Nally, bluntly say what they have to say, and the heck with you. I prefer the latter. "I'm glad for you and your wife. Now, that night, the night of the PTA. Did you leave the building and go anywhere except to your car?"

He pursed his lips and shook his head. "No. In fact, our minister, Reverend J. Harvey Wesley attended with us. He gave the invocation. He rode over with us, and we dropped him off at the parsonage after the meeting. You can check with him."

I jotted the name, and Seebell provided me his telephone number. I slipped the notepad back in my pocket and rose to my feet. "You've told me all I needed to know, Mr. Seebell." I offered my hand. "Thanks for your time."

He looked surprised, but rose quickly. "Is that all there is?"

"That's it."

"But, I figured . . . well, I don't know just what I did figure."

I explained. "Look. I've done a lot of work on this. I'm satisfied you couldn't have killed George Holderman that night." I didn't tell him that the only way he could have gotten to Holderman was by growing wings. I patted my pocket. "And if Reverend Wesley verifies your account of the evening, you're out of the picture."

He stared at me for several seconds. He released a long sigh. "Thank you."

I glanced at my watch as I left the pharmacy. Not quite nine-thirty. I had time to return to the office and type up my notes before lunch. When I climbed in my pickup, I pulled out my cell phone and put in a call to the Reverend J. Harvey Wesley, who verified the details Seebell had given me for that night.

Traffic was building on Congress Avenue. Parking spaces were at a premium, and often drivers parked in the outside lane, blocking traffic while they waited for a parked vehicle to pull away from the curb.

Deep in thought, I mulled over my progress. I had eliminated Frances Holderman, Fred Seebell, and Kim Nally, although the latter did have the opportunity. The algebra teachers, Saussy, May, and Flores provided what I figured to be indisputable alibis for each other, unless the three of them were in it together. That possibility I placed somewhere between being more powerful than a locomotive and leaping tall buildings in a single bound.

The two young men monitoring the hall claimed the three returned within minutes. Of course, I reminded myself, it doesn't take hours to smash a skull and plunge a knife into a man's chest.

I had only two suspects left, Perry Jacobs and Harper Weems. I still considered the latter was a long shot, so long I almost laughed at myself.

The truth of the matter was, I didn't believe there was any way Harper Weems could have pulled it off. Even if he could have somehow reached the second floor, how much leverage could he exert from a wheelchair to swing a ball bat?

I had covered every inch of the case, and no cigar. "So, Mr. Smart Private Eye," I muttered to myself. "Who did kill George Holderman?" I was aggravated and frustrated. I needed a new angle, and I couldn't find one.

Suddenly, I became aware of someone behind me honking. I looked in the sideview mirror and spotted a red Cadillac parked behind me, waiting for my spot. I couldn't make the driver out except it was a woman, and she was waving for me to leave.

I rolled down the window and waved her past.

A screech of burning rubber split the air, followed by a squeal of brakes. She had slammed to a halt beside me, an obese woman with frizzy blond hair. A cigarette dangled from her lips. She shook her fist at me. I couldn't hear what she was screaming, but I knew she wasn't wishing me a good day.

In the next second, she angrily floorboarded the red Cadillac. In a boil of blue smoke and spinning wheels, the large vehicle leaped forward.

Maybe God does work in mysterious ways, for scant seconds later, a parked vehicle pulled out, and our lady in the red Cadillac slammed into it, knocking it into the car ahead.

I laughed with glee, and as I drove slowly around the pile-up, I honked. When she looked at me, I waved my fist at her. It was a childish act, I admit, but I enjoyed it immeasurably.

Chapter Twenty-four

Back at my office, I made a few inquiries through Better Business and the Chamber of Commerce about Austin Expediters. The company was legitimate. I sighed with relief.

By mid-afternoon, another front accompanied by rain swept in. I left the office early, stopped in a local glass shop and had the windows replaced per my insurance agency's instructions.

Just after six, I pulled under the carport and dashed across the lawn to my apartment. Once inside, I turned up the heat, put a can of chili on the burner, and ignoring my pledge, popped a cap on a can of Old Milwaukee.

Then I fed the kitten. "Here you go, Cat. Chow down."

Beer in hand, I stared out of the window at the darkening sky. The rain fell hard, silver arrows pounding into the grass, exploding in the street. In the reflection cast by the window, I saw Cat gobbling his nuggets.

Abruptly, a black Lexus pulled up in front, and a giant unfolded from the front seat and lumbered up the sidewalk to my door. Godzilla aka Huey! And probably wearing a double-breasted Brioni suit under his raincoat.

The only reason I knew the suit was a Brioni is that was the only brand this particular Godzilla wore.

For a moment, panic threatened. Then I remembered. Danny O'Banion had invited me out to the County Line Barbecue for fat, juicy pork ribs and ice-cold draft beer along with a loaf of the County Line's home-baked bread.

The door groaned in its frame when Godzilla knocked. I opened the door and stared up into Huey's rock solid face.

"Mr. O'Banion sent me to get you," he growled in inimitable Neanderthal.

I gave him a weak grin. "Sure, Huey. Come on in. Let me turn off the stove."

Danny grinned at me when I slipped into the back seat. The infectious Irish grin topped by a tousle of red hair always put me at ease. "Tony, boy. How's the man?"

We shook, and he handed me a Bud Lite.

"Hanging in there, Danny. You?" One glance at his cashmere topcoat told me he wasn't starving.

He laughed. "You know me. Never look behind. Whatever's back there might be getting closer."

"Nice coat."

He grabbed the lapel. "Like it, huh? It's one of them Luciana Barbera things. And this suit"—he gushed—"it's a Nick Hilton. Fifteen hundred bucks at Barney's on Madison Avenue."

I nodded. "Nice." I glanced down at my washed out jeans and tweed jacket from JC Penneys.

The luxurious vehicle eased into the street, and I leaned back into the plush upholstery. I had forgotten the sensation of riding without bouncing.

The rain continued, a steady beat on the top of the car.

As usual, County Line was superb. We ordered the All-You-Can-Eat platter. With it came a loaf of freshly baked bread. As we gnawed through rib after rib and downed beer after beer,

Danny filled me in on Nelson Vanderweg and Villafono, aka Nelson Van Meyer.

"Van Meyer?" I wiped the barbecue sauce from my chin.

Danny switched a mouthful of ribs to his cheek. "Yep. But, the Oldsmobile is licensed to an Alice Baglino in Phoenix."

I frowned, but he continued. "Not to worry. I put out word. Just before I left tonight, I got the stuff for you. Villafono and Vanderweg are two of the aliases the guy uses."

"Two?" I poured another mug of beer from the frosted pitcher.

"And more. He's got a list the length of your arm. Ladies man. Loves them, then leaves them, but not before taking a sizeable portion of their bankrolls. Pretty slick too."

"Any warrants out for him?"

"Not in Texas. Arizona either. That's what I meant about him being slick. He knows just how far he can go."

I muttered a curse and tore off a chunk of meat from the bone savagely. That didn't surprise me. Not many women wanted to go on record that they'd fallen for some good-looking gigolo who cared more about their money instead of their body.

Danny studied me a moment. "Who's the guy to you, Tony?"

"Nobody." I shrugged. "Not really."

An amused grin played over his lips. "He get your squeeze?"

I shot Danny a murderous glare.

He chuckled. "Sorry. I remember your young lady. Rich if I'm not mistaken. Spoiled too." He turned his attention back to the platter of ribs.

We ate in silence for a few minutes.

"What do you plan on doing, Tony?" Danny's question was judiciously tentative.

"Beats me." I shrugged. "I guess I am a little jealous. Janice and I would probably never have married, but we had a lot of good times together. I don't want to see her hurt."

"Look, Tony. I don't want to fight with you, so tell me if I'm out of line, but how come this squeeze of yours is so—what's the word? You know—"

"Gullible? Trusting?"

"Yeah. Gullible. How come she's like that?"

I considered his question. "She's always had money. Hey, ten thousand to her is like ten bucks to me. She never worked for it, so she's got no idea of its value."

Danny shook his head and tore off a chunk of bread and sopped the sauce from his plate. He leaned forward and popped the bread in his mouth. Around the mouthful, he said, "Say the word. We'll send this bozo back to Arizona for you, Tony Boy. In a box."

I was tempted. But I resisted. "Thanks, but I figure this is probably something she has to find out herself. She needs some kind of closure. The guy just up and vanishes, she'll always wonder about him."

"What do you mean?" He frowned. "Wonder what?"

I pointed a dripping rib at him for emphasis. "You know, why did he go? Was it something she did? Should she chase after him?"

He cocked his head aside. "Why would she wonder something like that?"

I suppressed a chuckle. "Because she's a woman. Women wonder about things like that. A friend doesn't call her for a month, she thinks the friend hates her."

For several moments, he considered my explanation. Finally he shrugged. "Whatever you say."

Danny and I had one of those typical male friendships. Unlike the fairer gender, we could go months without seeing each other and take up right where we left off. I've no doubt if we showed up at a party wearing the same clothes, we'd throw our arms around each other and swagger around the rest of the night calling ourselves twins.

So, now our conversation ranged from sports to school days

to gossip to present plans. "What kind of job you got going now, Tony Boy? Anything exciting?"

"Exciting? Boring is more like it."

With a touch of amusement in his voice, he replied, "Come on, now. I figured you were leading the life of James Bond."

"In your dreams," I answered. "I've run into one dead end after another on this case. It's really got me buffaloed." I sketched out my investigation of Holderman's death, leaving out the details that were none of his business.

He pushed away his platter of rib bones and leaned back in the booth. "Who were some of your suspects?"

"No one you'd know." I shrugged. "Teachers mostly. Not all though." I named them.

He arched an eyebrow. "That last woman, Frances . . . I heard about her a few years back. If I'm not wrong, she turned tricks at some bar in Elgin. The others, those teachers, I never heard of except what's-his-name."

I was preparing to take the last bite of potato salad, but the fork froze inches from my lips. "Who?"

"Holderman. The guy who got whacked."

I tried to absorb his announcement. The two men moved in different worlds. How in the blazes could they have met? "George Holderman? How'd you know someone like him?"

Danny pulled out a pack of Marlboros and lit one. Inhaling deeply, he released a stream of smoke into the rafters. "He the one who was a big wheel in some school district around here?"

"Safford? Safford ISD. That one?"

He arched an eyebrow. "Beats me. But he's the one."

"Well." I leaned forward impatiently. "What do you know about him?"

He tapped the cigarette ash in his plate. "Not much. He's a small time butter-and-egg man, I hear."

His remark put a frown on my face. "A what?"

Danny grinned. "You need to get out on the streets more,

Tony boy. Butter and egg. A staker. He bankrolls the candy man." He shook his head wearily at the confusion scribbled across my face. "Pusher. Junk dealer. Candy man."

I understood, but all I could do was stare. Finally, I found my voice. "Holderman is a drug dealer? I mean, he was a dealer?" I tottered on the edge of disbelief.

Matter-of-factly, Danny replied, "No. There was no room for another one. One of the dealers lost his staker and found Holderman."

I still had a couple of uneaten ribs on my plate, but my appetite had vanished. I reached for my mug of beer and chugged it down. Without hesitation or any thought to AA, I refilled the mug. "How long had this been going on?"

He pursed his lips. "Oh, I don't know. Three, maybe four years."

I made a mental note of his last answer. "You know anything else about him?"

He shook his head. "Nope. Holderman was nothing. Sort of like a gnat hanging around on the edge of all the business. He probably didn't pick up more than four to six grand a month."

I did my best to contain my surprise. Six thousand a month. I thought of his estate in Brentwood Hills. Now I knew where the money came from.

Danny stubbed out his cigarette and added, "He's small change. His kind come and go."

If six grand a month was small change, I wondered just what amount Danny figured to be worthwhile. I shivered. Then an idea struck me. "Hey, Danny. You ever heard of a business called Austin Expediters? Delivery company of some sort."

He pursed his lips and shook his head. "No. Why?"

For a moment, I couldn't decide whether I should tell him about Stewart or not, but then, we went way back. "My cousin, actually, my cousin once removed, is working there. Three or four days now. I checked with Better Business and the Chamber of Commerce. It seems to be legitimate, but do you know if they're connected with the drug scene in Austin or not?"

A sly grin on his freckled face, he studied me a moment. "Worried about the kid, huh?"

I shrugged. "Not a kid. He's twenty-two, but yeah, I'm worried about him."

He grew serious. "I never heard of the place. That don't mean nothing, but when one does open up, I hear about it fast. This one, I haven't heard nothing. Don't sweat that one, okay?"

A thousand-pound weight was lifted from my shoulders.

Chapter Twenty-five

The rain had slackened to a drizzle by the time Danny dropped me off at my apartment along with a promise of our getting together soon. I agreed although we both knew soon could be a year from now.

Even before we left the County Line, I'd planned out my next few moves. As soon as I got back to the apartment, I'd put in a few phone calls, the first to Leroi to let him know Stewart was doing just fine. Afterward, I would follow Nelson Vanderweg/Villafono/Van Meyer home. I needed an address for what I had in mind.

My first call was to Arizona, to Wylie Carey, the manager of the Explorer Apartments in Phoenix.

A disgruntled voice answered.

I identified myself, reminding him of our earlier conversation about Vanderweg. "Yeah. I remember you. What do you want now?"

"You want to get your money back, Mr. Carey? Make him pay for trashing your place?"

"You kidding me? Just you tell me how."

"First, have you filed charges against him for trashing the place and threatening you with a lamp?"

"Naw. Started to, but I figured it was more trouble than it was worth."

"Every state's different. But, could be that you might be able to get a felony warrant on him. Maybe for assault. I don't know if you'd ever get your money back, but if you don't file, you sure won't ever have a chance to get it."

He hesitated. "Yeah. I know, but—"

"Look. This guy is a slick con artist. Comes in, finds rich women, wines and dines them, then skips out with a chunk of cash."

"So?"

"So? Besides me, has anyone else called for him?"

The sudden excitement in his voice told me he understood what I had in mind. "Hey, yeah. Yeah, now that you mention it, there was one woman who must've called a dozen times trying to find him."

I contained my own excitement. "By any chance do you have caller ID?"

"Sure. We get a lot of prank calls. Why? I . . . oh, yeah, yeah. I see what you're after."

"Right. If you can locate her, call me back. This is my home number. If I'm not here, leave her name and number on my voice mail. I'll contact her and try to get her to press charges against the guy. With two Arizona warrants on him, Texas can arrest him and send him back." I crossed my fingers that the name on his caller ID was Alice Baglino, owner of the beat-up Olds Vanderweg had traded in on the Mercedes.

"You really think so, huh?"

"I know so. Now listen. Here's what you've got to do. First thing in the morning, go down and file charges. Let me know what happens. Okay?"

Suspicious, he asked, "What's in this for you?"

"It's personal, Mr. Carey. Very personal."

After hanging up, I called the Ranchman's Motel in Amarillo. The motel had no caller ID nor a means of recording incoming calls. All my eggs were in the basket that Phoenix, Arizona was carrying.

It was 2 A.M. when Van Meyer left Janice's condo. He headed south on Burnet Road. I remained far behind, eyeballing his taillights and the silhouette of his car against oncoming lights. Once or twice, I cut into parking lots, made a loop and pulled back on the trail, hoping to give the illusion of one vehicle turning off and moments later, another pulling onto the street.

I didn't figure I needed to be so cautious because even early in the morning, Austin traffic was hectic. Still, I didn't want to take a chance.

And that's what caused me to first almost lose him, then barely miss jamming my bumper up his tailpipe.

The second time I pulled back onto Burnet Road, I glimpsed his taillights weaving through the traffic. "What the . . ." I muttered, wondering why he had sped up. Had he spotted me? Tightening my fingers about the steering wheel, I jammed the accelerator to the floor, and when the powerful Vortec 5.3 V8 engine kicked in, my pickup leaped forward.

Suppressing a curse, I squinted down the street, trying to pick out the Mercedes. Abruptly, lights flashed red just in front of me. I cursed, whipped to my right, honked, and flashed past the Mercedes. "Sonof . . ." Immediately, I turned right on Shoalmont Drive.

I glanced in my rearview mirror in time to see the black Mercedes pass the intersection. I took another left at the next corner and circled back to Burnet Road.

By now, I'd lost Vanderweg, or Villafono, or Van Meyer, or whoever the guy was.

Just as I passed the 45th Street intersection by the Texas State School for the Deaf, I glanced to my right. I jerked my head back around when I spotted a black Mercedes coupe parked next to a telephone carrel in the parking lot of a Big G Convenience Store.

Cursing, I pulled into the right lane and circled the block, coming back around to 45th just as Van Meyer sped past, heading west.

Eight or ten blocks later, he pulled into the Bull Creek Apartments. Talk about luck, I told myself. Bull Creek Apartments were leased for a minimum of six months. A lessee had to fill out tons of forms.

I parked down the street and, staying in the shadows, hurried into the parking area into which he had pulled.

"There you go," I muttered as he mounted the stairs to the second floor and entered his apartment. Minutes later, I slipped upstairs and made a note of his apartment number.

Back in my apartment, I called information and under new listings, found Nelson Vanderweg's telephone number. Next I booted up my computer and searched my public records databases for his social security number and birth date, both of which I knew I wouldn't find. They were as bogus as his name.

Sure enough, I didn't find them. So, I went to the web page of Eddie Dyson, computer whiz, entrepreneurial snitch, and local thief. I typed in my request for a birth date and social security number of Nelson Vanderweg, apartment 223, Bull Creek Apartments.

Eddie had forsaken the dark corners of sleazy bars for the bright lights of computers. Any information I couldn't find, he could. There were only two catches if you dealt with Eddie. First, you never asked him how he did it, and second, he only accepted VISA credit cards for payment.

And then I went to bed, knowing in the morning when I awakened, the information I wanted would be waiting. Thank God for technology and Eddie Dyson.

* * *

And it was.

Birthdate and social security number of Nelson Vanderweg. And Eddie only debited me $150. Probably because I gave him a lot of business.

Nursing a morning cup of coffee, I studied the monitor and jotted the information in my notebook. At eight o'clock, I would take my next step, although I hadn't decided exactly what I was going to do with the information.

While I waited, I perused the Denver white pages databases for Harper Weems' brother. "A name like that shouldn't be hard to find," I muttered, scrolling down the Ws. There were four Weems in Denver, one of whom was a woman.

As a consequence of surfing the web, examining various databases, and monitoring various chat groups, I developed a fairly broad network of contacts around the country. There were two PIs in the Denver area. I knew both.

I e-mailed DL Burnet a contract for frontal pictures of each of the three Weems to be e-mailed as an attachment. In addition, I requested he indicate each individual's dominant hand.

The next hour, I spent transcribing my notes and posting charges for Marty. He'd yell when he saw the bill from Eddie Dyson, but he'd be good for it. He had before. He knew that was one of the costs of doing our kind of business.

Finally, I pushed back from the computer and breathed a sigh of relief. I was caught up on the dreaded detail work. I was good at it, but I still hated it.

I pulled out my notes on Vanderweg and reached for the telephone. Time to play detective and see what other information I could dig up about him. If he followed his MO then he was milking Janice for all he could, and would do so until he slipped out in the dark of the night.

Even though she'd dumped me for Vanderweg or Villafono or Van Meyer, which made me not just a little jealous, I didn't want to see her taken to the cleaners. We'd had good times. And knowing her mercurial temperaments, we probably would again.

Donning the persona of Nelson Vanderweg, I dialed Southwestern Bell, explaining to the young woman in the billing office that although I had put down my deposit on the new service, I had forgotten to record it in my check register. "Could you tell me how much it was and the date I wrote you the check?"

She told me.

"Seventy-five dollars. On the tenth. That was almost a month ago. By any chance, can you tell me the amount of my next bill. I'll go ahead and send it in."

After a pause, she replied. "Seventy-three dollars forty-eight, Mr. Vanderweg. And the due date is the same day of the month, the tenth."

I thanked her again, broke the connection, and dialed Vanderweg.

A sleepy voice answered.

"Mr. Vanderweg. This is Charles Riley, service representative for Southwestern Bell. I am calling about your seventy-five dollar deposit. We have no record of receiving payment, and you have another bill in the amount of seventy-three forty-eight due in a few days. Unless we receive some kind of payment or you make arrangements to pay, we will be forced to discontinue your phone service."

He exploded. "What the . . . I paid you lousy . . ." He ranted and raved. "How do you think I got this telephone in the first place?"

I let him rage. After a few moments, I calmed him. "Look, Mr. Vanderweg. Why don't your look at your checkbook while I'm on the phone."

"You bet," he sputtered. "Just a stinking minute." Seconds passed, and he returned. "I've got it right here. I paid the deposit on November 10."

I played innocent. "You did? What was that check number?" I grinned to myself as he read it off. "What bank did you draw it on? And the account number please so we can locate it in our billing system. It was probably credited incorrectly to another account, Mr. Vanderweg. I'm sorry."

Gleefully, I recorded the data.

Now, with his account number, social security number, and birth date, I was ready for my next step, which was to call the automated line at his bank and enter the account number and his social security number.

The thin voice of the automated attendant replied. "The last deposit was November 18 in the amount of twenty-five thousand dollars. Four checks, numbers eight-seven-nine, eight-eight-zero, eight-eight-one, eight-eight-three cleared in the amount of four thousand two hundred and ninety-seven and twelve. The balance in the account is twenty-seven thousand four hundred and twenty-eight and thirty. Thank you. If you wish this message repeated, press two."

I whistled softly as I jotted the figures into my notebook. He hadn't wasted any time with Janice. I sat studying the figures, contemplating my next move. Should I show her what I'd dug up on the sleazeball? Or should I confront him?

Both questions were no-brainers. Neither would work. Either way, Janice would resent me for interfering. Of course, I reminded myself, with the Morrison fortune behind her, twenty-five Gs, even fifty wouldn't be missed.

"That's probably why the Lothario hooked up with her," I growled, puzzling over my next step, which I finally decided was to do nothing. Nothing, except wait and watch. Be patient until I heard from Arizona. At least, I could keep an eye on his bank account. The gigolo wasn't working, so it was safe to say that future deposits would probably be courtesy of the Morrison fortune.

Maybe if I was patient enough, I would find the opportunity I needed. I crossed my fingers.

But, for Janice's sake, I couldn't afford to be too patient.

I put in a call to the Travis County Hospital to check on Carrie Cochran's condition. She had a name for me, one that might break the case wide open.

She was still in ICU. "But her condition has been upgraded to guarded," a young nurse said.

Chapter Twenty-six

The phone rang while I was in the shower, but I couldn't hear it. When I padded back into the living room, the light was flashing. I punched the voice mail.

I grinned when I heard Wylie Carey's voice. "Got what you want. Alice Baglino." He gave me her number, and added, "She called sixteen times over a three-day period after that louse bailed out. I haven't called her. Figured you'd want to. As soon as I hang up, I'm going downtown to file charges."

I stared in disbelief at the receiver in my hand. Sixteen times! She must've really been hung up on the guy to call back so many times. I crossed my fingers that she had some kind of written proof of any money she had given him. If she did, then we could nail his sorry hide to the wall. If not, well, then we'd have to depend on the charges filed by Wylie Carey, the manager of Explorer Apartments.

I guess one of the reasons I felt as if I'd found my niche in the PI business is that I had a chance to stop some of the bullies of the world from running over those who were weaker. Not that I'm a do-gooder, but I don't like seeing someone having the screws put to them without some recourse.

Alice Baglino was at first reluctant. Naturally, she didn't

want word spread of how romantically foolish she had been, but when I gave her Vanderweg's background, which I shamelessly embellished with a lie or two, she agreed.

'Now, Miss Baglino. The money you gave him. Cash or check."

"Oh, check, of course."

"How much?"

She hesitated, then reluctantly answered. "Fifteen thousand." She hurried to explain. "He said he would invest it for me, but he cashed it and left. I know because when I got the check back from the bank, he had endorsed it and cashed it the same day I gave it to him."

A check. I wasn't sure just how Arizona law would view a check. Probably as a gift.

But then she made my day. "But I did write out the name of the company on the check."

That threw me. "Company?"

"Yes. You know, the company he said he was investing it in. Investment-Royals Incorporated. That was the name of the company, but when I checked, there was no such company in Walla Walla, Washington."

I resisted shouting for joy. "I think you have more than enough to file charges, Miss Baglino. I don't know how much of what you gave him you'll be able to get back, but if he wants any break at all with the law, he'll try to make some kind of restitution."

She hesitated, then added, her voice filled with pain, "I didn't have that much, Mr. Boudreaux. I had to quit work years ago to care for my ailing mother. We lived on her social security, and saved what little I made addressing envelopes at home. After she passed away, I was all by myself, and then I met Nelson. He was so gentle, and so understanding. I thought he was Mr. Right for me. I trusted him. Why, the day he disappeared, I even loaned him my car. He took it too."

"An Oldsmobile."

"Why, yes. A '95 model. How did you know?"

I ignored her question for the moment. "Did you sign over the title to him?"

"No, but it was in the glove compartment along with insurance and registration papers."

"Look, Miss Baglino. I know for a fact he had the Oldsmobile in Amarillo, Texas. He's driving a Mercedes now. I don't know if he sold your car or just left it next to the curb somewhere."

"But, he didn't steal it. I let him use it."

I rolled my eyes. Love made people do crazy things. And lonely people in love did even crazier things. "Yes, but maybe if you explain to the police that you expected it back in a few days, they can do something."

"Yes, but . . ."

"Look, Alice. This guy skipped out with a large part of your nest egg and your car. He has a history of taking advantage of"—I caught myself before I said 'lonely'—"of trusting women. If you don't help me stop him, he'll do it again."

There was a long silence at the other end of the line. Finally, in a soft, tremulous voice, she said, "You're right, of course. I just . . . well, you know, I just thought Nelson was different."

I grimaced when I heard the tiny tremor in her voice. "Look. Here's my home number. Call me after you file the charges. Then I'll start things in motion down here. I've got voice mail so if I'm out, just leave a message, okay?"

After hanging up, I leaned back and grinned smugly at the telephone. Surely, between Alice Baglino and Wylie Carey filing charges, we could nail Vanderweg.

The December weather turned unseasonably warm. To many Texans, Christmas was enjoyed in shorts and tanktops, and unless there was a big change within the next couple of weeks, that's how they would again gather around the table to fill their plates and plop down in front of the TV for the ball games. We did the same back in Louisiana.

I was in a sort of limbo, waiting for the attachments from Denver. Expecting no startling epiphany, I decided to spend the remainder of the day visiting the businesses George Holderman had inscribed on his desk pad. So before noon, I visited Hanks Barber Shop, the YMCA, Olympic Gym, and Luigi Liquors.

They all remembered George Holderman as a steady customer, a likeable guy, and a free spender. A regular guy was the consensus, a crying shame, the common accord.

As an afterthought, I asked about Harper Weems and Perry Jacobs. Hanks knew Jacobs as a customer. He'd never heard of Weems.

I had no better luck at the other businesses.

On the way home, I pulled into Lupe's Tacos on Ben White Road, a bright pink stucco structure with a red tile roof and sweeping arches. Inside, colorful piñatas dangled from the heavy black beams spanning the ceiling. An eclectic collection of bullfighting paraphernalia hung on the walls, toreros' swords, matadors' capes, picadors' lances, in the center of the rear wall hung a *Traje de Luces*, the suit of the lights, a colorful sequined suit worn by bullfighters. The shiny wood tables gleamed; the tile floors sparkled. Lupe's was a clean Tex-Mex restaurant.

I asked the young waitress who greeted me for the manager. Moments later, a smiling young Hispanic woman emerged from the rear. Dark complexioned with long black hair, she was a striking paragon of Hispanic beauty.

"Yes, sir. Can I help you?"

"I hope so," I said in my best little-boy-lost tone. "This just hasn't been my day."

"Maybe it'll change," she replied brightly, her dark eyes laughing.

I identified myself and showed her Holderman's picture. "A few years back he was a regular here. About once a month. Recognize him?"

The laughter in her eyes vanished, and the smile on her face faded, but while she quickly replaced the smile, she couldn't replace the laughter in her eyes. "I think so. But, I haven't seen him for a long time now."

"His name was Holderman. He died about a year ago." I glanced around the large room. There were only a handful of customers.

She shrugged. "I wish I knew more. I wish I could help you." There was no conviction in her voice.

I waited for her to continue, but after several awkward seconds of silence, I came to the profound conclusion she had said all she was going to say. "Do you know a man named Harper Weems? He's in a wheelchair."

A glimmer of recognition flickered in her dark eyes. "Oh, yes. He has blond hair. He has come out here before. He hangs around with the kids."

"Kids?"

She indicated the clock on the wall. It was three-thirty. "High school kids. They come here after school and hang around at night. He is a good friend of theirs."

"Did he ever come out here with Holderman?" I showed her the dead man's picture again.

"No." She shook her head. "I see them talk some, two, maybe three times, but the one in the wheelchair, he always came in his van. He is a nice man. I think he is one of the kids' teachers."

A voice called from the kitchen.

"One more question. What about a man named Perry Jacobs? You know him?"

She shook her head. "No. Sorry." She stepped back and cast a hasty glance at the diners along one wall. "I wish I could help, but if that's all, I need to get back to our customers and get ready for the afternoon rush. School is out."

I nodded, sensing the anxiety in her tone. She knew more than she was saying.

Chapter Twenty-seven

As I pulled out of the parking lot, two carloads of laughing teenagers pulled up and scampered inside. On impulse, I whipped my truck around and headed back to Safford High School. Maybe I could catch Harper Weems before he left.

Evidence doesn't lie. The problem comes when it is being interpreted. Too often, a zealous investigator forces the evidence into a pattern in which it doesn't belong. He manipulates it, not deliberately, but because of his perspective of the case.

I hoped I wasn't doing the same thing with Harper Weems, but something continued to nag at me about the man. Was it because the evidence overwhelmingly proclaimed his innocence? Yet, what did he and Holderman have going? Simply school? Impossible. He had deliberately lied to me, claiming the only time he had dealt with Holderman was at school, yet the waitress at Lupe's says she saw the two in conversation more than once and Holderman had written Weems' initials on his desk calendar on several occasions.

Engrossed in my own thoughts, I paid no attention to the black Camaro convertible behind me. If I had, maybe I could have stopped another murder. If I could have made the connection.

The high school was empty except for the school administrators and the sweepers, one of whom was cleaning around Harper Weems' desk when I arrived.

An older woman with thinning gray hair pulled back in a short ponytail, she told me he had left fifteen minutes earlier.

With a laugh, I replied, "Story of my life. Seems like I'm always fifteen minutes late." I introduced myself, explaining that the principal knew I was in the building. I glanced at Weems' desk, spotting a picture under the glass desktop.

She nodded knowingly. "Oh, yes. You're the one trying to find out who killed Mr. Holderman."

For a moment, her declaration caught me by surprise, and then I remembered. Not even e-mail travels as fast as gossip through the cleaning crew of a school building.

"Trying to," I replied. "I'd planned on asking Mr. Weems a couple of other questions."

Her face lit up. "Mr. Weems is a real gentleman. He loves these kids. He never gives up on them, even them what mess theirselves up with all them drugs."

"Yeah. That's what I've heard." On impulse, I tossed up a trial balloon. "I hear he spends a lot of time out at Lupe's Tacos on Ben White Road with the kids."

"I don't know about that place. But, he does go out and try to stop some of the kids from buying drugs. I never heard of that place though, but that ain't no surprise. Personally, I don't know why them kids go anywhere to buy drugs when they can get all they want right here at this school."

And she was right. I remember the locker searches, the drug dogs, the futile attempt to stem the flow of drugs through high school. Turn off one source, another was pumping away before you could spit. And to compound the problem, schools didn't want drugs to be discovered for fear of damaging the school's reputation.

"I hear Mr. Weems is a twin. He has a twin brother up in Denver."

She smiled broadly and pointed a wrinkled finger at a snapshot under the glass top of his desk. "Yes. Here's the two of them. Mr. Weems told me they took it last summer."

I suppressed the urge to shout. Maybe I hadn't been reaching too much. They were identical. Same color hair, same face, same shoulders. Put either one in a wheelchair and you couldn't tell them apart.

I thanked the sweeper and headed back to my truck, rearranging my neat little theories. I remembered Weems' hand when we shook that first day. It was soft, uncallused. No way a man can push a wheelchair for fourteen or fifteen years and have the heel of his hand soft and clean. No way.

Pushing through the front doors of the high school, I jerked to a halt. "What the . . . ," I muttered, breaking into a trot down the sidewalk toward my pickup, which sat forlornly on four flat tires.

The same grinning driver climbed out of the Riverside Salvage wrecker and shook his head at me. He pulled off his gimme cap and ran his fingers through his bushy red hair while he studied my truck. "For someone who ain't no teacher, you sure got on some kid's bad side, mister."

I looked back at the empty windows of the high school. "Friend, I got a feeling you're right."

Thirty minutes later, sporting four new tires and a $383.73 debit to my VISA, I pulled on to Highway 71 and headed home, mulling my conversation with the sweeper.

Could there have been some kind of drug connection between Harper Weems and George Holderman? Danny O'Banion identified Holderman as a staker, one who bankrolled the pusher. Could Weems be the pusher, the dealer? That would explain his visits to Lupe's Tacos despite the sweeper's observation that Weems was always trying to help students.

But, how did Weems pull off the hit? I was convinced he was indeed paraplegic, that it was a physical impossibility for him to reach the second floor.

The only answer was that Weems' brother could have taken his place that night. He rolled into the restroom, raced upstairs, whacked Holderman, then just managed to get back downstairs before Jacobs showed up. Jacobs had claimed he thought he saw someone disappear around the corner of the stairs. And Weems' room was at the very bottom of those same stairs.

On impulse I continued down Ben White to Lupe's Tacos instead of taking I-35 north to my apartment. I didn't expect to see anything at the restaurant, and I wasn't disappointed. "Probably too early for action," I muttered.

I headed back to my place, planning on an evening of typing notes and organizing my thoughts. In some of the popular fiction, I read about those guys with steel-trap minds, who can focus on half a dozen different ideas and follow through on all of them at the same time. I didn't believe it. I had all I could handle trying to keep focus on one thing at a time.

That's when Marty stepped in.

The voice mail on my telephone was flashing when I walked in. I glanced at the readout. Marty Blevins, 4:32 P.M. An hour earlier. "Now what," I muttered, wondering if he was going to praise or fire me.

I dialed the office, but he was gone for the day. I left a message on his phone, then called him at home. Still no answer. I left another message.

The attachments from DL Burnet, the Denver PI, were waiting in my mailbox, three professionally executed pictures of three different men, but one, Arthur Weems, leaped out at me.

Harper Weems' twin brother. Like the snapshot on Weems' desk, identical, except now the brother wore a burr haircut.

He was tall, a few inches over six feet, I guessed. He was climbing into a BMW that was parked in front of a sprawling building of Spanish architecture with a sign indicating it was the Rocky Mountain Country Club.

I cut my eyes to his wrists. A surge of excitement swept over me. He wore his watch on his right wrist.

Hurriedly, I skimmed the hard copy below the photo. Arthur Weems. Left-handed.

I pumped my fist in excitement. I was right. I was right.

Leaning back, I replayed my theory, rehearsing it for Marty. Weems dealt drugs to high school kids. Holderman was his staker. A dispute arose. Weems' brother came in from Denver, whacked Holderman, then headed back that very night.

I suppressed my excitement. "Easy, Tony, easy. Don't get ahead of yourself." I e-mailed Burnet a request for Weems' activities on November 11, 2004 and the source of his income. I reread the message before I sent it. "Come back right," I muttered, punching the send button.

Now all I had to do was find proof that Weems was a dealer. "That shouldn't be hard," I muttered, pulling my Fuji 35 from my desk drawer. I fit it with a 200-400mm zoom lens with a 2x tele-converter. With that rig, I could pick up a flea on the belly of a fly perched on a ten-story building. More than once on stakeout, I'd snapped incriminating shots that assisted our investigations. "Shouldn't be any problem now," I muttered.

I figured if I could catch any money or drugs exchanging hands between Weems and a student, I could pressure the student to come clean.

A sharp knocking on the door interrupted me.

It was Marty, cradling a paper bag in his arm like a baby. "I was heading home, so I thought I'd drop by for a talk."

"Sure. Come on in," I said, stepping back and opening the door.

Chapter Twenty-eight

He stepped inside and handed me the bag. "Bourbon. Figured we might as well relax."

Taking the bag, I led the way to the kitchen. "What's the occasion?" I gestured to a barstool and pulled out the bourbon. To my surprise, it was Jack Daniels. I poured him a stiff drink and ran a tumbler of water for me.

Puffing, he hefted his bulk up on the stool. "Concerned. Got a call from our client. She was upset about you questioning her."

I watched as he sipped his drink, trying to get a read on his thoughts, wondering if he was second-guessing himself about assigning me the case, wondering if he was second-guessing himself about even keeping me on his staff. "What'd she think? That I was going to forget all about her? Hey, she's the number one suspect with everyone."

He grunted. "Who knows what she thinks? She's our client."

I looked him square in the eyes. "I didn't do anything special with her. I questioned her just like I have all the others. And I did my best to assure her that it was just part of the routine. I've done my best, Marty. If you don't like it, then . . ." I left the rest unsaid.

With a frown on his forehead, he studied me. Finally, a faint grin broke the frown. "Hey, I know that. I just wanted to know what pushed her buttons. It's no secret the Safford police has her as its number one suspect."

I took another drink and shook my head. "I don't think she did it. But, here, let me show you why she got upset." I pulled out my notes. "I was going to type these up tonight, but now that you're here, you can see firsthand where the investigation stands."

In the next few minutes, I laid out my investigation of Frances Holderman, from exotic dancer to demure housewife. Marty almost choked on his drink when I dropped the bombshell about her looking for a hit man.

He looked at me in disbelief. "She what?"

"Yeah." I chuckled and refilled our glasses.

Frowning, he looked up from my notes. "How do you know she didn't do it this time?"

"Let me see if I can put this whole thing in perspective."

He gave his head a brief nod. "Yeah. I think I'd like to hear that."

I thumbed through my notepad for a clean page, which I ripped from the small book. "First, motive. Why was he murdered?" I jotted down each reason. Unfaithful, money, destroying a career, adultery . . . I could probably have named a dozen more reasons, but I had a gut feeling the real reason someone whacked him was because of the drug scene. To use Danny O'Banion's colorful description—a butter and egg man, a staker. "I think he had some kind of dispute with the dealer he backed. I'd planned on looking into that tonight."

Marty blinked, then shook his head sharply as if to clear his thoughts. "What about all those other motives? Why not one of them?"

"Opportunity, Marty. You see, there was only a handful of possible perps in that wing of the building. All access to that wing was either videoed or monitored by individuals appointed by Howard Birnam, the high school principal. Neither Frances Holderman nor Fred Seebell, whose wife slept with the superintendent, had the opportunity."

"What about those who did?"

"Good question. Kim Nally had the opportunity, but not enough of a motive. None in fact." I knew I was stretching the truth of my answer, but I didn't want to get into any sort of discussion with Marty tonight. I still wanted to get out to Lupe's Tacos and see if I could pin something on Weems.

"Of all the others in that wing, only one, Perry Jacobs, had both opportunity and motive. Personally, I don't think he was the one, but I can't prove it one way or another yet."

He frowned. The wheels in his brain turned slowly, crunching through the rust. "But, none of them had anything to do with drugs. I thought you said it was hooked up with drugs."

"I think it is. I'll know more after tonight. A little surveillance work. Cross your fingers that I'll have something to tell you in the morning."

He studied my notes a few seconds, then slid off the barstool. "Sounds halfway plausible to me." He paused at the door and glanced back. "And be careful tonight, you hear?"

Though the weather had moderated, the December night still carried a chill. I grabbed a threequarter-length topcoat and a heavy scarf, anticipating spending much of the evening outside.

Since someone at the high school obviously knew my pickup by sight, I parked in the shadows of a GI Salvage store a block away, and walked to Lupe's, cutting across the parking lots of the adjoining businesses, staying in the shadows as much as possible.

Next to Lupe's parking lot was one of those ubiquitous shopping centers thrown up in the sixties, a single-story stretch of brick with a dozen different stores. The strip center was the forerunner of the sprawling malls today. A portico ran the length of the center, in front of which was an ancient hedge of shrubs.

At the end of the shopping center nearest Lupe's, I found a

shadowy nook behind the hedge in front of a darkened real estate office. Behind me was an aluminum garbage can. The only way I could be spotted was if someone stepped on me. From my vantage, I had a clear view of two-thirds of the parking lot as well as the main entrance to the restaurant.

Several cars were already parked, some empty, others with two or three students inside and a few more with students leaning against them, laughing and joking. As I watched, a gaunt mongrel slunk from behind the office. When he rounded the corner and spotted me, he bolted across the lot to the rear of Lupe's where he sniffed his way around the dumpsters, searching for scraps of garbage.

Time dragged. The temperature dropped. I buttoned my coat snugly and squatted beside one of the columns supporting the porch of the real estate office.

More cars pulled in, new pickups, Fords and Chevrolets and occasional Dodge Rams. Several Toyotas, Nissans, Geos, and Camaros parked in clusters about the lot, the kids hanging their heads out the windows to visit before pulling into a parking slot and going inside.

The kids all appeared well-behaved. I saw no evidence of drug use. Glancing at my watch, I saw it was only 10:30. I snapped a few shots with my Fuji.

Thirty minutes later, Harper Weems parked his van in front of the restaurant. Moments later, the side of the van slid back and a silent lift lowered Weems and his wheelchair to the ground. He rolled himself inside Lupe's.

I muttered a curse. I couldn't see Weems' movements inside the restaurant, but I reasoned that he was too smart to deal in there. The parking lot was much better, much more private despite being in plain sight of everyone.

A black Camaro convertible pulled into the lot, parking near the highway under the tall marquee of the restaurant. As if on signal, a dozen more upscale BMWs, SUVs, Neons, and Firebirds screeched in, pulling in around the Camaro.

Leaning against the support column to steady the camera, I adjusted the lens for a clear picture of the group. They milled about the way high school kids do, joking, laughing, exchanging cigarettes, sipping from cans covered with insulators that not only kept the beverage cold, but unidentifiable from passersby.

To my surprise, I spotted Tim Briggs and Marvin Handwell in the group. They mingled, but neither appeared to be smoking nor drinking. I shot a few frames.

A few vehicles left, only to be replaced with new arrivals.

Then Harper Weems rolled into the picture, propelling himself across the lot to Briggs and Handwell. Adjusting the lens for maximum magnification, I snapped furiously.

Weems stopped in front of Briggs and extended his hand. At that moment, Handwell, of the mushroom haircut, stepped between me and Weems.

"Sonof . . ." I glanced left and right, but there was no place to move for a clear shot. Either way, I'd be in the middle of a parking lot, in plain sight for all to see. All I could do was cuss the boy. He'd blocked a shot of what appeared to be Weems attempting to hand Briggs a bag of drugs.

Finally Marvin moved, and I got a perfect shot of Weems offering Tim Briggs, the football star and National Honor Society member, a small bag of a white substance. "You sleazy . . ." I muttered between clenched teeth.

To my delight, Briggs obviously had rejected it for Weems pulled the bag away. "At least, some kids have brains," I whispered under my breath.

In the next instant, Briggs and Handwell climbed into the black Camaro and, followed by three other cars, drove across the parking lot in my direction, coming to a halt less than seventy-five feet away. Two hundred feet beyond, Harper Weems, still holding a tiny bag of a white substance, sat by himself in the middle of the lot, looking after the students who had left him behind.

Slowly, he propelled himself back to his van.

I shot another frame. "Serves you right, you no good sleazebag," I muttered, snapping one last shot as the van drove from the parking lot. At least, I had some evidence. Not absolute proof, but enough to start work on, enough to give some credence to my theory that Weems was the dealer, and Holderman had been his staker. Whatever the falling out between the two, I felt certain Harper Weems had enlisted the aid of his twin brother, Arthur, to carry out the murder of George Holderman.

Arthur could very well have been the one Perry Jacobs thought he spotted heading down the stairs. Harper could have even delayed Jacobs long enough for his twin brother to climb out a classroom window and disappear into the night.

I took a step back and hit the garbage can, knocking it over on the sidewalk. It sounded like someone banging away with a pair of cymbals.

As one, the cluster of students jerked around, staring in my direction. I pressed into the shrubs. After a short discussion, two beefy young men started toward me.

Frantically, I searched for an explanation. I had the distinct feeling "Just hanging out" wouldn't work. At that moment, the gaunt mongrel I'd startled early, sniffed past, paused at the overturned garbage can, and prowled for food.

"Hey." One of the boys laughed. "It was only a scroungy mutt."

"Yeah," the other one chimed in as they turned back to their friends.

At that moment, Briggs and Handwell climbed in the Camaro and drove away. For the next couple of hours, I huddled behind the shrubs as vehicles continued coming and going. Several times, I spotted drugs surreptitiously changing hands. Apparently, Lupe's parking lot was a local drug mall with no dealer having an exclusive on it.

The number of high school students remained fairly constant until just after 1 A.M. when, as if on signal, the group dispersed.

I dropped the film off at an all-night pharmacy downtown that offered one-hour delivery.

During the remainder of my drive home, I went over the case, searching for holes in my theories. Harper Weems was my prime suspect. All I needed was one or two witnesses who would swear Weems tried to give them drugs.

And the most credible witnesses were Marvin Handwell and Tim Briggs. I made a mental note to visit them at the high school the next morning. Once I had their statements, I could wrap up the case against Harper Weems.

I hesitated. "What if you're wrong, Tony?" I mumbled half aloud.

But I couldn't be. Oh, I knew some would think I was reaching too far, but the evidence seemed clear. First, Harper's twin was identical, and he was left-handed. In addition, he was a tall man, tall enough to deliver the blow at such the appropriate angle with the ball bat and to drive the switchblade into Holderman's chest.

Both brothers had money. While I had not checked their bank accounts, their creature comforts screamed wealth. The twin in Denver drove a BMW and belonged to a country club. And Harper lived in one of the most expensive condos in Austin, the Crystal Creek complex west of the city, a complex too expensive for a schoolteacher to lease. Hey, too expensive for a schoolteacher to even drive through.

And if the boys would admit Weems had attempted to sell them drugs, then I had a good case.

The only other suspect remaining was Perry Jacobs. He had both motive and opportunity. I still had a gut feeling he was innocent, but I couldn't prove it. And though I'm no brain trust, I was smart enough to realize that both Marty and the Safford police would focus their suspicion on Jacobs before Weems.

I should have felt smug about my neat little theory, but something nagged at me. I wasn't fooling myself that I had the case all wrapped up.

"But, listen Marty," I said to the empty seat next to me with the same emotion as if my boss had really been sitting there, "none of the others had reason . . . a real motive to kill the guy. Hey, on the surface, it might look that way, but that PE teacher for example. She had nothing to gain. Besides, she's a hard one. She doesn't look it, but she's hard as nails. She deliberately aborted. And Holderman's wife . . . she isn't stupid. Why kill the guy? As it was, she had money. She traveled. She had an itch, she scratched it. Why take a chance of losing all that?"

Taking a deep breath, I thought back over my little speech for Marty. If there were holes, he'd find them, but personally, I felt I had put together a solid argument.

Chapter Twenty-nine

I picked up the film from the pharmacy just after 7 the next morning and grinned when I spotted the shot with Weems offering Briggs a bag of drugs. "Now, I got you nailed, you sleaze," I muttered. "Try to get out of this."

Remembering my last two visits to Safford High School, I pulled around to the side of an Easy Time Convenience Store and walked the last three blocks to the school.

Principal Howard Birnam quickly accommodated my request to see the two young men. "You can use my office."

Five minutes later, the two young men entered the office. They hesitated when they saw me. I grinned and gestured to the chairs in front of the desk.

We made idle chitchat for a couple of minutes, and then I grew serious. "I'm here, boys, to ask for your help."

A momentary frown flickered across Briggs' face, then disappeared into a broad grin. "Sure, Mr. Boudreaux. Anything we can do."

Marvin glanced at Tim, then nodded eagerly. "Yes sir."

I slid a picture across the desk, the one in which Weems was offering Briggs a bag containing a white substance.

Marvin caught his breath and looked up at Tim in alarm.

The crewcut young man frowned. In a measured tone, he said, "You were at Lupe's last night?"

"Yeah." I glanced at Marvin, puzzled at the sudden agitation on his face. I shrugged it off.

Tim laughed. "Boy, Marvin. I didn't know you were so ugly." Marvin laughed with him. Tim nodded. "Yeah, that's us, Mr. Boudreaux. Us with our friends and Mr. Weems. So, what do you want to know?"

I pointed to the white bag in Weems' hand. "Is that drugs?"

Neither boy answered.

"After you boys left last night, I saw one or two other drug deals go down," I added, holding up the envelope containing the remainder of the exposures.

Marvin glanced nervously at Tim.

After a few moments of tense silence, I explained, "Look, what I want is for you boys to provide confirmation that Harper Weems was trying to sell you that bag of drugs."

Shifting his large frame in the chair, Tim looked me squarely in the eyes. "Why were you out at Lupe's last night, Mr. Boudreaux?"

I cleared my throat. "Sometimes, Tim, when we look into one matter, like the Holderman murder, we stumble across other problems. That's what happened here. I can't tell you who tumbled us to Weems, just like I won't tell anyone about you boys talking to me." I paused. "All I'm asking, guys, is that you confirm or deny that picture you're holding. Was Weems trying to make a sale?"

Marvin glanced briefly at Tim who studied the photo intently a few seconds longer. Finally, Tim spoke. "I don't know what to do, Mr. Boudreaux. I sure don't want to cause trouble for me or Marvin. You know what I mean? We got nothing to hide, but this . . ." He nodded to the picture. "And what you're asking is big time, at least for kids like us. You know?"

I knew I was asking a lot. I entreated them. "But, if we don't put him away, he'll continue selling the stuff. And not every young man or woman has the strength like you boys to say no."

The two young men exchanged looks. My request had disturbed Marvin, but Tim remained unruffled, though reluctant. He dropped his gaze to the floor, unable to meet my eyes. "I know what you mean, but, well . . ." His voice trailed away. He turned to Marvin. "What do you think?"

Marvin shrugged, keeping his own gaze riveted to the floor. "I dunno."

Tim looked back at me. I could see the indecision on his face. I knew, though, if Tim agreed, then Marvin would follow him. I hastened to add, "Look, boys. You don't have to decide now. Think about it. Talk to your folks. I'll guarantee you that Weems won't know a thing until it's too late. We don't need his kind around here."

Slowly, the crewcut young man nodded. "Yeah. Yeah, we need to talk to our folks, Mr. Boudreaux. Don't we, Marvin?"

"Huh? Oh, yeah, sure. We can . . . ah, can do that tonight."

"Great." I rose and offered my hand. "Thanks, boys. I'll get in touch with you in the morning, okay?"

"Yeah." Tim eyed me squarely. A faint grin curled his lips. "Yeah. In the morning." He glanced at his watch. "We get to school about seven or so. We can meet you out front. Seven-fifteen."

As I left the principal's office, a voice stopped me. "Mr. Boudreaux. Just a minute."

I looked over my shoulder as a familiar face approached from the open doorway of a nearby office. He stuck out his hand. "Jim Hawkins. You remember. You talked to me about George Holderman."

"Yeah. Yeah, now I remember." I shook his hand.

He glanced around at the students passing in the hallway.

"Look, I need to talk to you." He nodded to the door at the end of the hall. "Do you mind?"

"Lead the way."

Moments later, we stepped inside an empty classroom, closing the door and leaving the hurricane-level clamor in the hallway behind us.

He turned to me and said. "I know you've been talking to a lot of people, but there's one thing I didn't tell you about Perry Jacobs."

I arched an eyebrow. "Oh?"

"Yes. I didn't think about it. I guess because I was just trying to answer all your questions, and it never occurred to me that it might be important. At least it didn't until Perry told me that you still suspected him even after I told you he was in the boys' restroom with me."

"Yeah. That's right." I explained my perception. "The problem is that although you were in the restroom with him, he could have accompanied Holderman to the room, killed him, and then returned to the bathroom. Just to establish an alibi. You see what I mean?"

Hawkins nodded, his earnest face filled with concern. "That's just it. He couldn't have done that because I was walking behind the two down the first floor hall. I had just signed in with the boy in the hall when I saw Perry and George turn down the old wing. I was right behind Perry when he left Holderman and went into the boys' restroom."

For a moment, I stared in disbelief. Jacobs might still have the motive, but his opportunity had been blown sky high.

Hawkins frowned. "Am I right? Doesn't that mean he couldn't have done it, at least, the way you said?"

Slowly, I nodded, studying him closely. There were no telltale signs of lying, no shifting eyes, no dry lips, no nervousness, just a determined, yet concerned light in his eyes. "Why didn't you tell me that when we first talked?"

"You just asked me if I saw Holderman go up the stairs. I

didn't. As far as I know, he could have gone into Harp's room."

I studied the resolve in his eyes. I believed him.

And now I was left with one suspect, however inconclusive my theory.

Apparently, no one had discovered my pickup at the convenience store, so, smug with the knowledge that I had outsmarted the little vandals who had slashed my tires, I drove back to Austin with a conceited grin on my face, despite Hawkins' revelation about Jacobs.

I had a good feeling about the boys. They knew what had to be done, and I was confident they would do as I asked.

For the time being, I was at a standstill. I couldn't think of anything else I needed to do before getting the boys' decision. So I decided to see my on-again, now off-again Significant Other, Janice, and feel her out about her new beau.

He was trouble in Pierre Cardin shoes, and even though she had dumped me, I didn't want to see her taken for a chunk of money.

Janice Coffman-Morrison lived in one of those glass and chrome high-rise condos overlooking Town Lake on the Colorado River. While she never told me in the years we were together, I guessed her lease ran about five thousand—not a year, but a month.

As the only heir to the Morrison fortune created by the Chalk Hills Distillery, she could well afford the rent. I parked behind her Miata and knocked on the door.

She blinked once when she opened the door and saw me. For a moment, a fleeting moment, she was speechless. Then she regained her composure. "Why, Tony. What are you doing here?"

I laughed. "Just happened to be in the neighborhood. Thought I'd see how you were. After all, we just broke up. We didn't become enemies, did we?"

She laughed, like the tinkling of a silver bell. "Heavens, no, Tony." She opened the door wider. "Come on in."

Following her into the familiar living room, I felt like a stranger. She gestured to a couch and curled herself into an upholstered wingback. "Care for some coffee or tea?"

"Whatever's convenient." I gave her my most charming smile.

She rang a bell. "How have you been?"

"Fine. Working. Staying out of trouble."

For the next few minutes until the maid brought the coffee, we made idle chitchat, boring chitchat.

After sipping the steaming coffee, which as usual was too weak, I broached the subject, Nelson Vanderweg. "I hope things are going okay with you and Nelson."

She arched an eyebrow warily.

With a touch of innocence, I said, "I don't mean anything by that, Janice. I just want everything to be good for you. After all, you and me, we're still friends."

"Oh." She relaxed. Her brown eyes lit up and her face became animated. I'd forgotten just how attractive she was. "Oh, Nelson is the most wonderful man." She hesitated and shot me a quick look. Her cheeks colored. "What I meant was . . ."

I waved her embarrassment away. "Forget it."

The animation returned to her face. "Why, Nelson has been everywhere and done everything. His family in Montreal is very wealthy. Timber, he said."

I nodded as she continued gushing his praises, rattling off his accomplishments like a child playing Chopsticks.

When she paused for a breath, I asked, "So his family is in timber. Is that what he does?" I sipped my coffee, trying to appear guileless while directing the conversation.

"Oh, no. Nelson is in investments. Why, just before he came here from Miami, he brokered several seashore deals with some of the world's largest hotel chains." Her voice dropped to a whisper. "I promised Nelson I wouldn't repeat it, but you're different. I know you can keep a secret."

"Of course." I lied and leaned forward, at the same time wondering just how in the dickens Miami, Florida got all the way up to Amarillo, Texas.

"Nelson made over three million on his last deal."

I whistled. "He must have the touch. I wish I had some money to invest. Maybe I wouldn't have to keep working."

She set her cup on the end table and leaned forward. "Well, I did loan him some money. Nelson says he's closing the deal next week, and my money should show a good profit. If it does, I plan on investing more with him. You can too."

Sitting there watching her, she reminded me of a foolish little girl giggling over her first boyfriend. I wondered if she had ever giggled over me like that. I made a pretense of looking at my coffee. "Oh? How much would I have to put up?"

Her voice took on the confident tone of a knowledgeable businesswoman. "I gave Nelson twenty-five thousand. He'd probably take as little as ten thousand because you're my friend. I can ask him."

That's mighty white of him, I told myself, resisting the urge to turn her over my knee and spank her silly little derriére. "He's closing the deal sometime next week, huh?"

She nodded emphatically. "Yes. Nelson said he could probably double my money."

I feigned surprise. "In just a week?"

"Oh, no. I gave him the money two weeks ago."

"I see." I nodded knowingly, trying to keep the sarcasm from my voice. "Three weeks. That's still pretty good."

She gushed. "Oh, Nelson knows exactly what's he's doing."

I could believe that. I don't know what that Lothario said or did, but he really swept her off her feet. "Sure looks like it."

"If you want, I can ask Nelson about investing some of your money."

The last thing I wanted was for Nelson to become suspicious.

I shrugged it off. “Oh, don’t bother. I don’t have anywhere near that kind of money anyway. Besides, you said he didn’t want you to say anything about it. I sure don’t want to cause any problems between you two. Just forget it, okay?”

A tear glittered in her eyes. “That’s sweet of you, Tony.”

“Yeah. I’m a sweet guy. Well, I’ve got to be going now.” I placed my empty cup on the coffee table and rose. “I’ve enjoyed our little visit.”

“Me too, Tony.” She jumped to her feet and took my arm. “You must come back again. I’m glad you came.” She hesitated, then looked up at me. “And Tony?”

“Yeah.” My eyes met hers.

“I want us to always be friends, forever and ever.”

Janice always had a knack for the melodramatic.

In my best Mike Hammer imitation, I touched the tip of my finger to her chin. “You bet, kid. You bet.”

I slammed the pickup door and stared at the condo. If I planned on saving her some money, I’d better get off my tail.

Chapter Thirty

Outside, the wind had switched to the north, pushing in a heavy cover of leaden clouds, marking the leading edge of another cold front.

I turned onto Lamar and headed for the office.

The Christmas spirit filled the streets with brilliantly trimmed trees, dazzling arrays of flashing lights, and occasional displays of reindeer.

Not quite two weeks to Christmas. I could already smell the rich aroma of baked ham, the pungent bouquet of rice dressing, and the sweet fragrance of pecan pie all mixed with the hickory piquancy of woodsmoke.

Years back, I had been an avid hunter and fisherman. In Louisiana, you ask a Cajun the four seasons, he'll tell you winter, spring, summer, and hunting.

Texans were the same. The rugged hill country northwest of Austin was rich with game, and the rivers and lakes abounded with fish. But, as I grew older, life somehow got in the way, and time grew between my periodic hunts until now my only hunting was with my cousin, Leroi, during Christmas in Church Point.

Actually, hunting is a generous interpretation of our annual venture. We'd take a blanket and a portable TV along with a container of medicinal whiskey to our respective stands to ward off snakebite, cold, and boredom in that order. After a couple of hours, one of us usually found his way to the other's stand and we spent the rest of the day discussing snakebites and reminiscing on years past while herds of deer and coveys of quail strolled idly by our stand.

Now, that's my kind of hunting.

In the office, I typed my notes, updated my reports, and filed my expense account. Marty was out, so I left my work on his desk.

If Tim Briggs and Marvin Handwell agreed to help, then the next morning by 7:15, I'd be ready to turn over all that I had learned to the Safford police. I could still be wrong. My case still had a few holes, but it was a heck of a lot tighter than any of the evidence against the others.

Just as I started to leave the office, my phone rang. I hesitated, then shrugged. Why not? Maybe it was American Publishers calling to tell me I'd won $10 million in their giveaway.

No such luck. It was Marty. He was at the police station with Chief Ramon Pachuca. "Chief Pachuca's asked me about the Holderman case. If you're not tied up, how about coming down and filling us in on where we stand?"

I cussed under my breath for picking up the receiver. I should have known better. I took a stab at getting off the hook. "I told you last night, Marty. It's about the same."

"You had a stakeout last night, didn't you?"

"Yeah, but. . . ."

"Then tell us about that." His voice was growing testy.

I wanted to beg off, but, Marty was boss, and Pachuca was too valuable a contact to blow off. I put on a happy face and cheery voice. "Sure, Marty. Be down in a few minutes."

Grabbing my report from his desk, I cursed all the way to my Silverado.

The temperature had already begun to fall. The cloudbank to the north was dark and ominous, promising a chilly night.

The station was crowded with the afternoon shift coming in. I nodded at a few familiar faces, stopped to chat with one or two, then made my way to the chief's cramped office where he and Marty waited.

Marty snorted. "You get lost or what?"

I winked at Pachuca. "Or what."

"Huh?" Marty frowned.

"Traffic. It's bad out there." I grinned. "You're our local law, Chief Pachuca. You oughta do something about all the traffic."

Pachuca leaned forward, chomping on his ubiquitous cigar, a cheap, thick roll of tobacco with a horrible stench. "Hey, the more taxpayers in this city, the more money. Suffer like the rest of us."

Marty grunted. "Where are you on the Holderman thing?"

I handed him the report. "I just finished this."

Pachuca leaned back, his eyes narrowing. "So?"

I studied him. I knew exactly what he was wondering. "Frances Holderman ain't crying that he's dead, but she didn't do it. She had motive, but no opportunity. Besides, she's too short, and she's right-handed."

With a grunt, Pachuca rocked forward. "What do you mean, no opportunity?"

Quickly, I explained the video camera used by the band directors. "Like most videos, it has a clock in the corner."

"Clocks can be changed," Pachuca growled.

"Why would the band director change it?" I paused, then continued. "From the time the PTA meeting was over until the body was discovered, she never came out the front door nor went down the hall. And neither did Fred Seebell."

"Seebell?" Pachuca frowned.

"Yeah. Holderman had an affair with Seebell's wife a few years back."

He arched an eyebrow, but said nothing. I reminded myself

that he and Holderman had been acquaintances. They had worked on a few committees together.

I continued. "Kim Nally, the PE teacher, had the opportunity, but not the motive. Like Frances Holderman, she's too short, and she's right-handed."

Marty pulled out a cigarette, paused and glanced at Chief Pachuca. Pachuca nodded, and Marty lit the cigarette. He blew out a stream of smoke. "No motive? Didn't he jilt her?"

"She aborted. Her choice." I explained how she had instructed George Holderman to find someone who would suck the kid down the drain, so George went to his wife, who could have applied for a patent on abortions.

Looking over my report, Pachuca asked about Perry Jacobs.

"No way. He was with another teacher in the restroom. The teacher swears it."

He eyed me skeptically. "You been showing how none of these suspects could have done it. Did you find anyone who you do suspect?"

"Yeah." I nodded to the report. "I didn't put it in there because I've still got a few unanswered questions."

"Well, who is it?" Marty leaned forward.

I looked from one to the other, wondering just how my theory was going to sound. With a sigh, I barged ahead. "Harper Weems. He's in a wheelchair."

The chief looked at Marty in stunned disbelief, then turned back to me. "Well now, Tony, I'm going to be real interested in just how he managed to get to the second floor."

Quickly, I explained. "He has a twin brother, identical. Now, I found out that Holderman was a staker for some drug dealer—"

Pachuca cut me off sharply. "Holderman was what? What in the blazes are you saying?"

"You heard me."

He snorted. "Where in the name of—" He sputtered. "Where did you pick up nonsense like that?"

Marty's eyes rolled about in alarm.

"Danny O'Banion. You know Danny O'Banion, don't you? Austin's gift from the Mafia or Costa Nostra or whoever."

Pachuca's eyes narrowed. He obviously didn't appreciate my attempt at humor. "You got that from O'Banion?"

"Yeah." I waited for him to respond, but he remained silent. I took that as a sign of grudging respect for O'Banion's street smarts. I continued. "Holderman was the staker. He bankrolled Weems who was the dealer."

Marty started to protest, but I held him off with a stay of my hand. "Hear me out. Now, I have photos of Weems trying to sell drugs to some high school kids last night."

Pachuca yanked the cigar from his lips. "You what?"

I held up my hand again. "Photos. Pictures, but I can't prove there were drugs in the packages unless the two boys he was hitting on will admit it. Two high school boys. Good kids. National Honor Society and football players. He was trying to sell them some, but they refused. I'll find out in the morning at seven-fifteen if they'll be willing to cooperate."

With a snort, Pachuca glowered at me. "You got shots of bindles changing hands?"

"Yeah." I handed him a photo. "At Lupe's Tacos out on Ben White, right here in Austin."

He stared at the snapshot. "Can you prove that bag contains drugs?"

"No. But, I might be able to in the morning. Like I said, that's when I talk to the boys again."

Before either could speak, I continued. "Here's the way I see it. Access to the room where Holderman got whacked was limited. A video camera from outside shows no one entering the wing. Two students monitored the hall, having everyone who entered sign in as the district required. No one else entered the wing. The only one who had opportunity, motive, and the physical requirements is Harper Weems . . . at least, Harper Weems' identical twin."

I leaned forward, trying to lay my theory out convincingly for Pachuca. "First, Weems deals. The picture confirms that. Second, his brother lives in an expensive condo, drives a BMW, and is left-handed. In addition, he's a tall man, tall enough to have slammed the baseball bat into Holderman's forehead at the precise angle and afterward, drive the switchblade in Holderman's chest. The two brothers work together. I don't know, maybe the brother deals up in Denver. Anyway, Weems and Holderman had a falling out. His brother comes in, offs Holderman, and disappears. Perfect. After all, there's no elevator up to the second floor. How can a crippled guy get up there and back so fast? The only answer is that the killer wasn't crippled."

Marty's frown deepened, but a faint grin was beginning to curl Pachuca's lips. "You mean," said Marty, "you mean Harper Weems isn't crippled?"

"No. He is crippled. I saw the x-rays. Talked to the doctor. The guy is a paraplegic. He'll never walk, which gives him the perfect alibi."

Pachuca squinted at the ceiling. "So, what you're proposing is that Harper Weems called his brother in, and when he knew Holderman was alone upstairs, sent his twin brother up." He paused. I could see the gears turning in his head. I wondered what holes he had found in my theory. "Okay. Say it was the brother. Holderman was in this room when all of a sudden, here comes a teacher who's been in a wheelchair for years, except now, he's walking and carrying a baseball bat." He shifted his cigar to the other side of his mouth. "Hey, he's witnessing some kind of miracle here that'll put Lourdes to shame. He'll have a thousand questions. And keep in mind, you only have the time it takes that Jacobs guy to use the bathroom, then walk upstairs." He glanced at Marty. "What? Three-five minutes?"

Marty shook his head and snorted. "I figured it was too good to be true."

I grinned. "But what if Holderman was facing the desk, and the killer was hiding in the closet?"

Pachuca frowned. "How do you know he was facing the desk?"

"No defensive bruises on his forearms, which there would have been if he had not been surprised."

Marty sputtered. "But—"

Chief Pachuca held up his hand. "Hold it, Blevins. Tony's got a point. A good point. It coulda gone down like that. The killer in the closet, then sneaking up on Holderman."

"Right," I replied. "When he turned, the bat was already descending."

For several moments, Chief Pachuca considered my theory. Marty eyed me skeptically, then turned his attention to Pachuca. Personally, I think Marty got lost after I mentioned the video camera. The only thing he picked up on was when Pachuca pointed out the flaw in my theory.

Pachuca shook his head. "I think you're stretching it, Boudreaux. How do you know it was the brother? Weems could have been in it with anyone. Why the brother?"

"Probably because Weems could slip his brother into the school easier."

"How?" His eyes glittered with amusement.

"The window. He opened the window."

"Couldn't he have done that for anyone?"

Marty frowned at me again.

"Sure. And his accomplice could have been someone else, but keep in mind. Whoever it was had to be as tall as Holderman, about six-one or so, and left-handed. The brother is both."

"He could've found someone like that."

"Yeah, but he couldn't trust him like he could his brother. Besides, if anyone saw him in the wheelchair, they'd think it was Harper Weems. People would notice a stranger. Who would be more natural a partner for a twin than his own identical twin?"

Pachuca arched a skeptical eyebrow. I continued. "Look,

Perry Jacobs claimed he thought he saw someone running down the stairs. He followed, but at the bottom all he found was Harper Weems." I paused. "What if it was the brother in the wheelchair. As soon as Jacobs went back upstairs, he could have slipped out the window."

For several seconds, no one spoke. Pachuca studied his folded hands. Marty studied Pachuca. I studied both. "Look, maybe it is farfetched, but we know the profile of the killer. None except Weems' brother meets it. If you eliminate those who did not have the opportunity, then the only one left is Harper Weems' brother, or someone of the same profile, like you suggested." I paused, took a deep breath, and fell silent.

Pachuca eyed me narrowly. "You're supposed to meet with those two boys in the morning?"

"Yeah."

After several seconds that seemed like hours, Pachuca nodded. "Give me a call after you meet with the boys. I'll meet you out at Safford. We'll sit with Billy Vanbiber. Show him what you got, and let it go from there."

Marty grinned up at me. I winked at him.

"Sounds good to me, Chief," I replied. "Mighty good."

Chapter Thirty-one

I felt pretty smug during the drive back to my place. I'd put together at least a tolerable case against Harper Weems. A few holes here and there, but at least I'd put together enough of a case that Chief Ramon Pachuca was willing to pitch in.

The phone rang as I walked in the door.

It was Alice Baglino in Arizona. She had filed charges, grand theft, against Nelson Vanderweg. "Now, what do I do?" Her voice quivered with uncertainty.

I tried to calm her nerves. "Just be patient now, Alice. I'll let you know when we're ready to move."

"Will it be long, do you think?"

From the inflection in her voice, I could tell she was having second thoughts. "No. Not long. Before Christmas."

She laughed nervously. "It can't be soon enough for me."

I laughed with her. "Don't worry. It'll all be over before you know it. And then it will be worth it. I promise you."

After she hung up, I sat staring at the receiver, trying to decide if I should take my next step now or wait. I really wanted to see just how Janice's investment turned out. Would the guy skip with her twenty-five Gs, or milk her for more?

The gray kitten rubbed against my ankles. Absently, I picked him up and scratched the back of his neck. He purred softly.

I thought about Alice Baglino. She was nervous. Obviously, she was not a confrontational person, and the enormity of her action frightened her. What if Nelson was extradited, and she dropped the charges? The guy would vanish faster than my old man could down a can of beer.

The smart move was to wait until the call from Phoenix, the call telling me that Wylie Carey of Explorer Apartments had indeed filed charges as he promised. Then I could move in confidence, knowing I had two shots at Vanderweg, knowing that the judge had two shots at him. And if Alice Baglino knew someone else had also filed against the creep, then she wouldn't be as likely to change her mind.

My stomach growled, and I remembered I'd skipped lunch. The coffee at Janice's had filled me up, and I'd been too busy with the reports, and convincing Chief Pachuca to give me a hand.

Except for beer, a half stick of margarine, a jar of pickles, and a slice of dried bologna curling up at the edges, the refrigerator was bare.

"Well, Cat," I muttered, holding the tiny kitten up to my face. "At least you have something to eat. I've got to go to the store."

I called Travis County Hospital after pouring Cat some nuggets. Carrie Cochran remained in ICU. And still no visitors. I crossed my fingers. But a nagging spark flickered to life in the back of my head. What if the name she supplied was not Harper Weems?

I shook my head. "It has to be."

The night was raw. A fine mist decided to join the chilly air, and between the two, even the short walk to my pickup left me shivering. I flipped on the heater, and within four or five blocks, warm air began filling the cab. Cold weather had always been courtbouillon or gumbo or stew weather in my family. I decided to whip up a pot of beef stew with thick gravy. Hot stew over steaming rice would take the chill out of anyone's bones.

Usually, I shopped about once a month, stocking up on nutritious staples such as beer, chips, lunchmeats, TV dinners, ketchup, and whatever happened to appeal to me as I pushed the cart down the aisles. I even picked up food for Oscar, my little Albino Barb exotic fish, when he was still alive. This time, I picked up a couple of cans of Fancy Feast cat food for Cat. Any items I needed in between, I purchased at a local drive-in.

Once back at my place, I tossed my coat on the couch, flipped on the TV, put rice on to steam, fed Cat, and then whipped up a chocolate-colored roux.

Roux is the Louisiana secret of delicious gumbos, jambalayas, courtbouillons, stews, and etouffees.

Roux

4 tablespoons flour
2 tablespoons vegetable oil
1 sautéed large onion
1 chopped bellpepper

Stir CONSTANTLY over medium flame until chocolate colored. If it's black, it's burned.

Add 4 cups water to roux

Then for the beef stew.

2 pounds of prime beef, 1-inch cubes.
2 onions, sliced and sauteed
1 16-ounce can tomatoes
2 celery tops, diced
2 large potatoes-cubed

1 teaspoon salt
1 teaspoon thymne
1 teaspoons hot pepper sauce
4 cups water
3 tablespoons roux

Boil beef cubes for thirty minutes, Until tender, then add remaining ingredients and simmer for one and a half hours.

Serve over steaming rice.

Now steaming hot beef stew can only be fully appreciated with an ice-cold beer. That being the sacred tradition, I did not consider imbibing a can as a violation of my efforts to stay away from alcohol.

So, with beer in hand, I carried a plate of steaming rice smothered with succulent beef stew and spiced with several shots of Louisiana Hot Sauce into the living room where I plopped down on the couch just as one of my favorite old flicks, *The Maltese Falcon*, came on cable.

"Well, Cat," I said, glancing at the kitten who was sitting on the coffee table, sniffing my bowl of stew. "Cold outside. Warm inside. Good food, good beer, good company, a good movie, and tomorrow, nail the lid on the Holderman case. What more could I ask for?"

Just then, a local news bulletin interrupted the opening credits of the late movie.

A grim-faced reporter stared at the camera. Behind her, lights flashed in front of an apartment complex. The wind whipped her blond hair in her eyes, and she drew her shoulders together in an effort to ward off the cold. "Tonight," she began, "a teacher in a nearby school district was found dead in his apartment by one of the maintenance men at Crystal Creek Complex. Less than an hour ago, Amal Washington discovered schoolteacher Harper L. Weems dead in his condo at this exclusive complex. According to Mr. Washington, it appeared Weems had been stabbed several times. He was pronounced dead at the scene. Investigators have no comment."

The reporter continued, but I heard nothing. My ears roared. I stared at the blurred images on the screen in disbelief.

Abruptly, the daze enveloping me shattered when I saw Chief Pachuca, wrapped in his topcoat against the weather, stride purposefully from one of the condos.

Several reporters converged on him. He waved them away and continued his hunched-forward, headlong stride to his cruiser.

I stared at the plate of beef stew on the coffee table in front of me. I pushed it away. For the first time in over forty years, I had no taste for stew.

Nor for beer.

The only drink that could handle the news of Weems' death was bourbon. I poured four fingers, downed it, and poured four more. The idea of getting stinking drunk suddenly took on a new appeal for me. For the last few months, I had been fairly temperate, which doesn't mean I laid off the booze the way I had promised AA, but that I didn't get falling down drunk. So maybe I was entitled. I knew I was rationalizing, but I didn't care.

The shattering jangle of the doorbell followed by a pounding at the door brought that idea to a screeching halt. I yanked the door open, and my jaw dropped open.

Standing in the door, soaked to the skin, his teeth chattering and shivering uncontrollably, stood Stewart Thibodeaux, my cousin. "Tony," he mumbled. "I . . . I . . ."

His words galvanized me into action. I pulled him inside. "Get in here, Stewart, quick. Get out of the weather."

He stumbled in, shivering and dripping water on the floor. His teeth chattered as he hugged himself. "I . . . I'm freezing."

"Stop talking. Get out of those clothes." I tossed him a towel and rummaged up some of my sweats. "Here. Put these on."

His whole body shivered as he managed to slip into the thick sweatshirt and pants.

"Drink this," I handed him my tumbler of bourbon.

He downed it in one gulp while I retrieved a blanket from the bedroom and proceeded to wrap it about him. He plopped on the couch and hunched over, trying to contain what little heat his body was generating.

Hurrying into the kitchen, I returned with a plate of stew. "Here. Eat some of this."

With shaking hands, Stewart managed to gulp a few bites, and slowly, his trembling body relaxed. Only then did I ask, "What are you doing out in this weather without a coat? You get sick, son, your daddy'll kick my rear."

He squeezed his eyes shut and pressed his lips together.

"Stewart? What's wrong?"

Finally, he shook his head and forced a weak grin. "Just cold, Tony. Left my coat back in the apartment." He hesitated, then added, "then my car broke down a couple of blocks from here. I can't get it to the shop until tomorrow, so I figured I'd spend the night here, if you don't mind."

Something didn't sound right, but I decided not to push the issue. In the morning would be time enough. "You're welcome here anytime, Stewart. You know that."

Chapter Thirty-two

I awakened with Harper Weems still on my mind. Rolling groggily from bed, I stumbled into the living room and jerked to a halt when I saw the couch on which Stewart had slept was empty. "Stewart?" I glanced toward the dark kitchen. "Where in the . . . ," I muttered, turning on the kitchen light.

The only room left was the bathroom, and it too was empty. Muttering a curse, I dialed his cell phone. No answer, so I left voice mail, a stern rebuke for his not telling me he was leaving.

Dressing quickly, I scoured the neighborhood for several blocks in every direction, but I couldn't find his Pontiac. Maybe he called a wrecker after I went to bed, I told myself. "But that makes no sense either," I mumbled as I headed for Safford High School.

The drizzle had stopped, but the clouds remained.

Tim Briggs and Marvin Handwell were leaning against the railing on the front steps of Safford High School when I drove up at 7:15. They cut across the lawn toward me. The boys wore tight jeans, Polo shirts, and letter jackets.

I remained beside my truck and waved.

They waved back, but there were no smiles on their faces.

"You heard about Weems, huh?" I said when they stopped in front of me.

Marvin scuffed the toe of his Nike running shoe in the gravel. "Yes, sir. I couldn't believe it."

"Yeah," said Tim. "Why, I saw him in the hall just yesterday in that squeaky wheelchair of his."

"Me too," said Marvin. He looked up from the ground at me. "Sure hard to believe."

"That's what you get when you mess with drugs, boys." I hesitated, chastising myself. This wasn't the time to preach.

Tim cocked his head to one side. "You think it had to do with drugs, Mr. Boudreaux? Really?"

"I don't know, boys. Honest. But, to be truthful, I don't know what else could have caused it. Drug dealers have short lives. Sooner or later, a bigger one moves in and decides to take over the turf. Something has got to give."

Marvin kept his eyes on the ground. Tim shook his head slowly. "I don't guess we can help you now, huh, Mr. Boudreaux?"

"On the contrary boys. Just because someone killed Weems doesn't change what went before." I hesitated. "Sure, now that he's dead, the drugs will stop out there, but I still need to confirm what the picture showed, that he was trying to sell you drugs. There won't be any publicity, any notoriety, nothing that will cause you any problems. I promise."

The boys exchanged looks. They conversed with typical high school dialogue, furrowed brows, wrinkled foreheads, shoulder shrugs, and mumbled words, all various attributes of their cryptic conversation. Tim turned to me. "Well, I don't suppose with Mr. Weems dead now there will be any commotion. Yes, sir. Mr. Weems did try to sell us drugs, crack."

I suppressed a shout of glee. I remained serious. "Had this started just recently?"

"No, sir. This is my fourth year at Safford. He was selling it when I came here."

Marvin nodded his agreement. "But, he never tried selling any to me until last year."

Tim shot him an angry look.

"Well, it's true," Marvin answered defensively.

The crewcut young man shrugged. "I know it is." He turned to me. "Is this all you need, Mr. Boudreaux. I hope you don't want us to sign anything. I don't know if my parents would let me do that."

"No, boys. That isn't necessary. I'll pass word on, and probably someone from Austin PD will contact you for a statement."

"Austin?" Tim glanced at Marvin. "You mean, it really doesn't have anything to do with Mr. Holderman's murder?"

I hated lying to the boys. After this mess was all over, I'd buy them a hamburger or something and apologize. "That's what I said, fellas. This is an entirely different matter from Holderman."

I pulled onto Highway 71 and called Chief Pachuca on my cell phone. He was his usual self, abrasive, belligerent, and cranky. "Well, Boudreaux, you took long enough to call." Before I could reply, he continued. "I guess you heard about Weems. So much for that farfetched theory you been dreaming up."

Ignoring his sarcasm, I asked, "Can you tell me anything about what happened?"

He snorted. "You know better than that."

"Well, what about yesterday? You said if the boys confirm Weems was a dealer, you'd help."

"Did they?"

"Not five minutes ago. Both of them. Weems had been dealing at least for four years." I hesitated. A sudden feeling came over me, a feeling that one piece of my puzzle had popped out of place.

Chief Pachuca continued. "All right. I promised. Tell you what. Drop by Safford PD. Tell Billy Vanbiber I sent you. Fill him in on your ideas. He doesn't want a case like Holderman's open. Maybe he'll want to follow through."

"Thanks, Ramon. I owe you."

Clicking off the cell phone, I laid it beside me on the seat. First crossover I came to, I headed back south on Highway 71.

I crossed my fingers that Billy Vanbiber would pursue the matter, at least to the satisfaction of the Universal Life Insurance Company. If they paid off the eight million to Frances Holderman, then Blevins Investigations would get its fifty thousand, plus expenses.

Chief Vanbiber was a lanky, rawboned Texan who looked as if he belonged on a horse, not behind a desk. Redheaded and freckled, he grinned easily. When I told him what I had, he jumped on it.

If my report had been a football, I figured Vanbiber would have tried to run it back for a touchdown. Quickly, I briefed him on what I had put together. Whether he actually saw the logic and motivation in my theory or whether he simply wanted someone to blame, I had no idea. I'd like to think he considered my collection of evidence and subsequent deductions a brilliant piece of police work.

For the next hour, I went over and over the report with him, answering each of his questions, explaining my own reasoning, and attempting to justify the conclusions I had drawn. To my disappointment, the longer we discussed the case, the less enthusiasm he seemed to show.

Just before lunch, he leaned back and steepled his forefingers under his bony chin, staring at the report on the desk. "You know, Tony. You've done a lot of work here, and I want to go along with you. It'd sure make my job a little easier, but the truth is, there's too many holes in it."

Before I could argue, he continued. "First, let's take Danny O'Banion's word that Holderman was a staker. Now I know O'Banion. And he's probably right. But where's the proof that Holderman was Weems' staker? He could have bankrolled someone else. Second, where's the proof Weems used his brother, or anyone else, to carry out the murder? Sure, you have a snapshot and two boys' word that Weems was a dealer. But, the way I see it that's all you have. Nothing more."

Hopefully, I leaned forward. "Don't you think it's worth following up on?"

He grew reflective. After several moments, he replied, "You might find something, but I can't see how it's worth the time for me to put one of my men on it. We've got too much else on our plates."

I grimaced, disappointed. As badly as he wanted to solve the case, I figured it was hard for him to back away from it. But, I didn't have to back away. "Suppose I can come up with a definite drug connection between Holderman and Weems. Would that be enough for you?"

A wry grin curled one side of his lips. "You're a stubborn cuss, aren't you?"

I chuckled. "My grandpa farmed rice. You want to see stubborn, you watch a Cajun farmer growing rice. Gambling with God, that's what my grandpa always said."

With a short nod, he pushed himself to his feet. "Find me a connection, Tony, and I'll jump in alongside of you."

"What the heck, Tony," I muttered as I climbed into my pickup and started the engine. "You knew you had a couple of big holes. Why are you so disappointed?" Pulling onto Highway 71 and heading north, I chided myself. "Stop griping and start working. All you have to do is connect Weems and Holderman."

And I knew just how to do that.

Danny O'Banion's office was on the entire top floor of the Green Light parking garage a few blocks west of the convention center in downtown Austin. The elevators opened into a reception room about twenty feet square. A single desk sat in front of one of the undecorated walls, which were covered with an off-white fabric. I felt like I had stepped from one elevator into a considerably larger elevator.

The soldier who had escorted me into the lobby pressed a button next to a stainless steel door, which slid open, revealing a spacious office with an expensive and tasteful décor. I knew Danny must have hired someone to decorate his office. His taste was about like mine, vintage Appalachian.

I paused as the door slid closed behind me. Danny came from around his desk with a grin so wide on his face that all his freckles ran together. I gestured to the office. "Hey, Danny. Think this is big enough? Why you can play football in here."

He laughed and took my hand. "You can, but you better not." He pointed to a chrome and glass end table. "This is a Lillian Gray . . . or maybe it's Eileen Gray." He shrugged indifferently. "I don't remember. All I know is that, it set me back a buddle." He gestured to the rest of the furniture with a broad sweep of his arm. "The decorator called the rest of the stuff Le Corbusier and der Rohe. You know, high-class items."

The names meant nothing to me. The last time I prowled about a furniture store was with my wife, Diane, now my ex. We furnished a small apartment in classic discount house. Two years later at our divorce, she took over sole possession of the furniture, sending me on my way with Oscar, my tiny Albino Tiger Barb, and his mates in the small aquarium. "Nice," I muttered. "Nice."

"How about a drink?" He stopped at the bar next to a span of windows overlooking the city.

"Thanks. Just water."

He arched an eyebrow as he poured me a tumbler of water and two shots of bourbon for him. He motioned to a couple of leather-covered chairs next to a window. "Sorry I don't have a platter of barbecue ribs for you," he laughed, referring to our last get-together out at the County Line Barbecue. "Now what can I do for you, Tony boy?"

"You remember Holderman? You said he was a staker?"

"Yeah." He nodded. "Right. So?"

"Can you find out if there was a connection between him and a dealer named Weems?"

Danny arched an eyebrow. "Weems? That the same one in the papers this morning?"

"Yeah." I eyed Danny closely. "The same."

"This still part of that case you were working on?"

"The same. I got two students who said Weems tried to peddle them some crack. If I can come up with some kind of substantiating evidence to support the boys' word, Safford police will put a man on the case."

Idly, Danny studied his glass, swirling the ice cubes through the golden bourbon. "The guy's dead, Tony. What good will it do?"

I stared out the window over the city skyline against a backdrop of dark clouds. The sight at night with lights sparkling and glistening was dazzling. Austin was growing like a healthy teenager, gobbling up land and daily adding muscle and strength to its burgeoning limits. I remembered Carl Sandburg's poem, *Chicago*. That city had nothing on Austin.

I turned back to Danny. "It's for our client. She has to have her name cleared to collect the eight million insurance on her old man. She collects, we make fifty Gs. I get ten percent of that. That's it, pure and simple. Like you say, the guy's dead. I don't really care about him now. Just our client."

He shook his head and gave me a wry grin. "At least you're honest. Sure. I'll see what I can find out."

I leaned back and grinned. "Thanks."

He grew serious. "Don't get your hopes up. Truth is, I've never heard of that Weems guy peddling."

With a frown, I leaned forward, trying to force the answer I wanted. "Yeah. But you don't hear about all of them, do you?"

"No. But one peddling from a wheelchair? Hey, Tony. Everyone would hear about him. And I never did. But, like I said, I'll ask around. Truth is, old friend, I think you made a bad bet on this guy."

"I hope not, Danny. I sure hope not."

I was subdued as I headed home. If Weems wasn't peddling, then what was he doing at Lupe's with Tim and Marvin? Exchanging recipes?

My cell phone rang. It was Stewart, apologizing abjectly for leaving that morning without a word. "Let me make it up to you, Tony. Let's you and me have dinner tonight. What do you say? You know Jimmy's Crab Shack on the Colorado River?"

"One of my favorites. What time?"

"Eight all right?"

"Eight it is."

Chapter Thirty-three

My phone was ringing when I opened my apartment door. "Hello."

"Tony. It's me, Janice."

I stammered. She was the last person I expected to call me, and for a moment, I was thrown off balance. "Janice? Is that you?"

She laughed, that same bright tinkling giggle of hers. "Of course, silly. Didn't I just say so?"

"Sure. Sorry. My mind was a thousand miles away. What's up?"

Her voice grew excited. "Nelson closed out the deal I told you about yesterday." Her tone grew confidential. "You know that twenty-five thousand dollars I invested?"

A sickening feeling grew in the pit of my stomach. "Yeah. Yeah. What about it?" I prayed she'd lost it all and had sworn never to invest again. Naturally, I was wrong.

"Tony, I made fifteen thousand. In just three weeks. Isn't that wonderful? Isn't that marvelous?"

I didn't want her to become suspicious, so I tried to be enthusiastic. "That's great. He must sure know what he's doing."

"Oh, he does, Tony. He does."

"That's great." I didn't know what else to say.

"And Tony, guess what?"

The hair on the back of my neck bristled. "What?"

"Nelson already has another deal. This one even better than the first."

I was suddenly wary. "What kind of deal?"

Almost apologetically, she replied, "I don't really know. I didn't ask." She paused, and then in a breezy tone, added, "Besides, what does it matter? Nelson knows what he's doing."

"Still—"

"Look, Tony. I know you said you couldn't put the money together, but that's why I called you. We've been friends for ages. I'll be happy to loan you the money to invest. When you collect your profits, you can pay me back. Then you can use those profits to keep investing." She paused.

I suppose if I'd been the kind to grow teary-eyed, I would have at that moment. A surge of gratitude warmed my blood. "That's very thoughtful of you, Janice, but I can't."

"Please, Tony. We need to act fast. Nelson says there might not be very many more opportunities like this one."

I bet there won't be, I growled to myself. "Thanks, but I can't. Of course, I'm thrilled for you."

"It's so exciting. You've no idea."

Trying to be nonchalant, I said, "So, how did you feel when Nelson handed you a check for your investment? How much altogether? Forty thousand?"

"Oh. He started to write me a check, but then he suggested I invest it in this next deal of his. There are plenty of investors, and I was lucky to get in on it."

I winced, desperately trying to figure out how to get her money back before it was too late. And from the way she talked, too late might already be here. "You mean, you invested the whole forty thousand?"

"Yes, and I gave him sixty more. That's an even one hundred

thousand. Can't you just imagine how much I'm going to make on that? Aunt Beatrice will be thrilled."

I would have collapsed if I hadn't already been sitting. All I could do was roll my eyes. Her Aunt Beatrice, CEO of Chalk Hills Distillery would be anything but thrilled. "You . . . you've already given him the check?"

"Oh, yes. He's already deposited it."

That sorry . . . I tried to sound upbeat. "Well, I wish you all the luck in the world. So, when does Nelson plan on making the investment?"

Bubbling with excitement, she replied, "I don't know. I heard him talking to someone, and he mentioned tomorrow at two o'clock."

I did some fast thinking. Sixty thousand. Even if he deposited the check this afternoon, the bank won't dare permit any fund withdrawal until a check that size cleared. That gave me a few more hours to figure out what to do. "Well, I'll keep my fingers crossed for you."

"That's sweet of you, Tony. Now, you're sure I can't loan you some money?"

"Yeah. I'm sure, but thanks. I appreciate the offer."

I hung up and sat staring at the receiver for several minutes, searching for an answer to the predicament. Sometimes a person struggles and battles for an idea that never comes. Other times, the notion just pops out of the clear. That's what happened to me. I knew exactly how I was going to take care of Nelson Vanderweg. And at his own game.

Reaching for the telephone, I called Wylie Carey at the Explorer Apartments in Phoenix, curious if he had filed charges.

Carey answered. I identified myself. "Just wanted to find out if you decided to go ahead and file charges against Vanderweg."

He didn't answer for a few seconds. When he did, his voice was tentative. "Yeah. Yeah. This afternoon. In fact, I just got back a few minutes ago."

"Great. Any problems?"

"No. Of course, I was kinda nervous. It's the first time I'd ever done anything like that. With the police, I mean. They weren't sure if they wanted to accept the charges, but they did. Aggravated assault."

"Good. I . . ." I hesitated. "Did you say aggravated assault? I thought you were just filing assault charges? Where did the aggravated come from?"

He hemmed and hawed a few seconds. I could hear the reticence in his voice when he finally replied. "Well, look. It's kinda a long story."

"Fine. Tell me. After all, we're working together on this. I'd like to know if there's anything that could affect what we're doing."

A trace of bravado edged his voice. "Well, I didn't tell you the whole story when we first talked, but when I went to collect for the damages and back rent, he grabbed a lamp and took a swing at me. It just hit me a glancing blow, but it scared me enough that I ran from the apartment. When I went back, he had split." With a tone of I-dare-you-to-disagree, he added, "And that's what I told the cops. They accepted the charges. Like you said, it's up to you now."

You listen to liars long enough, you acquire the knack to spot them immediately. Wylie Carey was a liar. I'm a terrible gambler, but I would have given 100-1 odds he had fabricated the aggravated part of his story. I played along with him. All he had told me was that Vanderweg threatened him with the lamp. Nothing more. No swinging or anything.

He was lying, but I didn't care as long as I nailed Vanderweg. "I guess I misunderstood. No matter. I'll take care of things here."

"Good. So, now what do I do?"

With a rueful grin, I said, "Just wait, Mr. Carey. Within a couple days, you'll have your money or your pound of flesh."

He was in for more than he suspected. Van Meyer aka Vanderweg would deny the act, and both men would be questioned. And one thing I found out, cops don't like being lied to.

I replaced the receiver and stared at it, rethinking my next step.

Dinner that night with Stewart took me back to the days when his daddy and I ran around together. He rattled on at the proverbial mile-a-minute telling me about his job and the future.

I was thrilled for him, and the first thing I did when I got back to my place that night was call his dad. In the background, I heard Stewart's mother, Sally, squeal in delight.

"Looks like things are going our way, huh, Tony?" Leroi said.

"You bet, bro. You bet."

Chapter Thirty-four

Just as I pulled into the parking lot outside our office the next morning, my cell phone rang. It was Danny O'Banion. More bad news. "Sorry, Tony. There ain't a soul on the streets seen anybody in a wheelchair peddling."

I muttered a curse. "They sure, Danny? Austin is a mighty big place."

He chuckled. "Tony, there's half-a-dozen peddlers working around Lupe's. They got their own little fraternity, like you college boys say. And no cripple in a wheelchair was part of it. Now, they've seen him out there, but he was with the kids. Sorry, old buddy. I know that isn't what you wanted to hear, but that's the scoop."

I stared across the parking lot, trying to reassess the case. Weems had been my last shot. With nothing to tie him and Holderman together, I knew no help would come from the Safford PD.

Holding the neck of my jacket tightly around my throat against the chilling wind, I hurried into the building. There was still Weems' brother. I held doggedly to the belief I had interpreted the evidence correctly. And if I had, then my theory was sound.

I placed another call to the Travis County Hospital.

Carrie Cochran had died at 3:32 that morning. So much for the name she was going to supply me.

I gave Howard Birnam a ring, but he was out. His secretary told me that Weems' body had been taken by Olsen Funeral Home.

Another call gave me the time set aside for viewing of the body. "Today and tomorrow. Eleven until five."

Then I got a surprise when I asked about the funeral.

"The family requested the body will be transported to Denver, Colorado for final interment," responded the polite secretary.

I never could understand the term, final interment. Wasn't interment final in itself? I've attended fifty or sixty funerals although I understand the older one becomes, the number of funerals attended increases exponentially. But of the fifty or so I had attended, not one host was later exhumed and moved.

One fact was certain. I was going to the funeral home. I had to meet Weems' brother.

Olsen Funeral Home was a sprawling white-brick, single story with a porch spanning the front supported by Doric columns. Twenty to thirty vehicles were parked in the adjacent lot.

Inside, three doors opened off a spacious lobby, each to a chapel. A bronze stand next to one door held a printed card, Harper Jerome Weems.

I hesitated when I entered the chapel. The walls were covered with photographs Weems had taken. Students filled the seats, lined the walls, clustered in small, serious groups. Many studied his photographs, somberly pointing out individuals within the prints.

The open casket rested on a maple bier at the front of the room. From there, it would be transported to the waiting hearse. At the head of the casket stood the spitting image of Harper Weems; his brother, Arthur. The only difference was that he wore his hair close-cropped. The viewing line stretched to two-thirds of the length of the room. I took my place at the end of the line.

Looking over the roomful of saddened students, I couldn't help being impressed by their obvious sorrow and grief. Girls sobbed aloud when they viewed the body. Silent, macho boys wiped furtively at the tears on their cheeks.

In a flash of awareness, I knew Harper Weems was no dealer. Even in a world of skewed and misplaced loyalties, no drug dealer could command the amount of emotion so obvious around me.

Still, I wanted to meet Arthur Weems.

Across the room, Principal Birnam and I made eye contact. Attired in a neat, dark blue suit, he smiled briefly and made his way through the crowd to me.

"How are you?" He extended his hand.

He really wanted to know what I was doing there, but like most of us, good manners forbade his asking. So, I answered the question for him. "Pay my respects. Weems must have been a good teacher. Besides, I wanted to meet his brother."

Birnam stood with his hands folded in front of him. "He's a fine man. I'll introduce you."

"Thanks."

We both fell silent. Somehow, discussing a murder at such a time seemed inappropriate.

Birnam broached the subject. "How's the investigation going?"

I eyed Arthur Weems and shook my head. "Not so good."

He grimaced. "Sorry."

The line shuffled forward slowly.

The funeral home did a good job on Harp Weems. He was one of the few corpses I had seen who indeed looked as if he were sleeping. At first glance, his long blond hair looked like a halo about his head.

Birnam introduced me to Arthur Weems. He smiled grimly and extended his hand. I couldn't help noticing the gold watch on his right wrist.

I expressed my condolences. At that moment, luck, which generally treated me like a mongrel dog, decided to throw me a bone.

"Thanks." He rolled his shoulders and grimaced. Looking around, he whispered to Birnam, "I could sure use a smoke."

Trying not to appear hasty, I pointed to the rear door. "Out back."

He hesitated, looking over the crowd.

"They'll be here when you get back. Trust me."

He grinned at the wry smile on my face. "I know." Turning for the door, he added, "Bad habit to have, cigarettes," he said, leading the way.

Birnam and I followed.

Outside, we made idle chitchat, the focus of which was Harp Weems. Arthur laughed. "Yeah, that brother of mine was always getting himself hurt. It got so I hated to leave the country. Seems like every time I came back, he was in some hospital somewhere."

I tried to be casual with my questions. "You travel much?"

He shook his head in despair. "All the time. I just got back from Saudi Arabia six months ago."

Six months? I had the feeling the few fragile remnants Danny O'Banion had left me of my Weems theory were about to be completely shattered.

Birnam asked the question I had planned to ask. "What were you doing over there? Harp never said."

"Oil. I'm an engineer. Exxon. My company sent me over for eighteen months." He took a deep drag and blew the smoke into the air. "I tell you true, friends. Even in the American compounds, Saudi Arabia ain't like home."

"Eighteen months?" I felt the breath go out of me. That meant he was out of the country in November 2004 when Holderman was murdered, which in turn meant my neat little theory about Harp using his brother to kill the superintendent had fallen flat on its face.

"Yeah." He grimaced. "And next month, they're sending me to Albania."

Birnam cocked his head. "Oh?"

"Afraid so."

I shut out their conversation. Oh, I'd check on Weems' claim that he was in Saudi Arabia, but I knew deep down that he was telling the truth. I cursed under my breath. I'd come a full circle again. Back at the beginning without a glimmer of who murdered George Holderman.

Next thing I knew, Birnam was shaking my shoulder. "You okay?"

Both men were looking at me with concern. "Huh? Oh, yeah. Yeah. I'm fine."

Weems flipped the cigarette through the air. "Well, time to return to the wars." He laughed. "By the way, you're more than welcome to the memorial service day after tomorrow at Harper's condo. Seven o'clock. Casual, punch and snacks. Tell a few lies about my brother." He grinned, but pain filled his eyes. "He'd tell 'em if he were here."

We left Arthur at the casket, shaking hands, accepting condolences. Howard gestured to some of Harp's glossies on the walls. "He had a knack with a camera."

Idly, I glanced at the photos, all in black and white. I'll give him this, he was eclectic. His prints ranged from sports to theater to academia.

I tried to visualize him in his wheelchair and the contortions he must have gone through to shoot from some of the different angles. There were some overhead pictures of various theatrical plays, ground angles of classrooms, and a mixture of various slants and perspectives of the school, the bank, the community.

I recognized some of the teachers; Kim Nally, Perry Jacobs,

and Henry Bishop. Then there was one of Rita Viator sitting at her desk in the counselors' office.

Tim Briggs and Marvin Handwell were easy to spot in the football pictures. One spectacular shot had to have been taken with a monster lens from the end zone for it depicted Briggs throwing out his right arm for balance as he released a pass to a fleet receiver far downfield.

Yeah, Harper Weems had a knack for cameras. For all the good it did him.

Disappointed and disgusted, I headed back to the office, trying to rearrange my broken puzzle. I refused to admit I was whipped, but every alley I turned down ended in the proverbial brick wall.

It's a cliché, but it is the truth. Misery does love company. Utilizing my shaky and questionable Biblical knowledge, I took that cynical observation one step farther, bad news begats bad news.

I had no sooner walked into the office than the phone on my desk rang. It was Janice. She was so wired, she could have lit a light bulb if you could find some way to screw it in her ear.

"Nelson says this deal is fantastic, Tony. He says I can double my money in two weeks. I just had to call back and see if you had changed your mind. This is a fantastic opportunity, and I hate to see you pass it up."

"Sounds exciting, but no thanks. By the way, did you ever find out what he's investing in?" I glanced around the office. Two of the guys were busy at their desks across the room.

"No. But whatever it is, it must be important. He wants me to meet him at his bank with the sixty thousand in cash."

"Cash? I thought you gave him a check."

"I did, but he called me back. Seems like the deal is moving faster than he thought. He can't wait for the check to clear, so he wants cash. We'll deposit it in his account tonight. That way, he can draw on it immediately if he has to."

There was no doubt in my mind he was planning on moving fast, like the next morning.

Janice interrupted my speculations. "Tony, are you sure I can't loan you some money?"

My brain whirled furiously. "Yeah, yeah," I replied almost absently. "But thanks again."

"Okay. But don't forget, I asked."

"I won't."

I depressed the release button and called National Security Bank, once again using the automated line in bookkeeping. When prompted by the computerized voice, I entered his account number and his social security number. The hesitating, synthesized voice of the computer replied. "Account number four, six, nine, three, zero, eight, one, one, dash, zero, one, eight, nine, two has a balance of eight thousand, five hundred, fourteen dollars and thirty-three cents. Thank you for using National Security."

I resisted the impulse to thank the machine.

Replacing the receiver, I pondered the information. $8,514.33. Where was the forty thousand, Nelson?

I knew where it was. Why was I asking?

Uttering a curse, I punched in Eddie Dyson's number. Eddie, a perfect example of modern business and graft adjusting to the Internet, surprised me by answering immediately. We exchanged pleasantries and then in a lowered voice, I told him what I wanted. "I plan to give a con man a taste of his own game. I've got all the information, bank account number included. I want to transfer a sum from one account to another. In the morning. Before the bank opens. Can you do it?"

"Nope."

I frowned.

But he continued. "However, I know who can."

"Who?"

Eddie chuckled. "Forget it, Tony. You go through me. How much you talking about?"

I glanced around the office again and cupped my hand over the mouthpiece. "I was hoping for eighty-five Gs. It'll probably be closer to seventy," I said, adding the sixty thousand deposit to the current balance.

"Cost you ten percent."

"That's good for me, Eddie. There was supposed to be a hundred in there. The guy's probably spent most of it. Get all that you can."

"You got it. Ten percent of whatever we can get."

"Yeah."

"Now, who's the guy?"

I gave him all the information. "And transfer it to Robert Rodison at the same bank, National Security. I'll call you back in fifteen minutes with the account number."

There was a short pause as he took the information. "Okay, Tony. You want me to put it on your VISA?"

I laughed. "What else?"

After I replaced the receiver, I rummaged through my desk for my stack of ID cards. I pulled out the driver's license and social security card for Robert Rodison. By a strange coincidence, my picture happened to be on the driver's license.

From time to time, we all have to stoop to devious methods, but then, it's the bad guys that force us.

Fifteen minutes later, I had the account open with an initial deposit of two hundred bucks. Outside, I called Eddie on my cell phone and gave him the account number.

Now, all I had left was to put in the call to the Travis County Sheriff's Department and have them pick up Nelson Vanderweg.

Chapter Thirty-five

I sat in my Chevy pickup in the National Security bank parking lot while I called the sheriff's department. I identified myself. "There's a runner in town."

Under his breath, he cursed. "Another one."

Ignoring his disgusted remark, I continued. "Two Arizona warrants on him, aggravated assault and grand theft. His name is Nelson Vanderweg, apartment 223, Bull Creek Apartments." I provided them the telephone number of the apartments plus the manager's name, knowing they would verify Vanderweg's presence before taking another step.

"You can contact me at Blevins Investigations or at home." I gave them both numbers. "I think the guy is ready to fly. Probably tomorrow. No telling where he'll light."

I clicked off the cell phone. "So much for your sorry tail, Vanderweg."

Shifting into gear, I headed for the nearest McDonald's for a traveling lunch, visualizing the unfolding scenario at the sheriff's department. At that moment, the Travis County Sheriff's department was calling Phoenix, Arizona to confirm the warrants. With the confirmation, the sheriff's department would pick Vanderweg up, take him before a judge, and then pop him behind bars to await an Arizona lawman to take him back.

I chuckled. Couldn't happen to a more deserving guy.

Back at my desk, I spent the rest of the afternoon juggling and rearranging my notes on the Holderman case. Finally, I reconciled myself to the fact that Weems was in all probability not responsible for Holderman's murder.

If only I could have spoken with Carrie Cochran.

Woodenly, I reviewed my list of suspects, carefully jotting down evidence that failed to support their complicity even though I had it all memorized by now. Kim Nally, PE teacher: Too short, right-handed, too weak, no motive. But, she had the opportunity. Perry Jacobs: Too short, right-handed. He had motive, but no opportunity. Frances Holderman and Fred Seebell had no opportunity. Both the band camera and the two young hall monitors verified that fact.

With a sigh, I leaned back in my chair and tossed my pen on the desk. I was exhausted. My head hurt. And I was confused.

Before I went to bed, I checked my e-mail. The Denver PI, DL Burnet, had sent me the information I requested. If there had been any question about Arthur Weems' part in the murder, the message blew it into a million pieces. Weems was where he had said, Saudia Arabia, from December 2003 until May 2005. Threequarters of his income, as did Harper Weems', came from a family inheritance.

Driving south in the heavy traffic on Lamar the next morning, I replayed the investigation over and over in my head, searching for some piece of evidence I might have misinterpreted, some scrap I could have misjudged.

Though I had not given Marty any false hopes, he would be ticked off. Either he'd fire me or I'd end up back at my old job running down skips and serving warrants. Maybe that's where I belonged. Maybe I would never be as successful as Al

Grogan, the number one honcho at Blevins Investigations. Maybe in the grand scheme of life, I was destined to be mediocre.

Of course, I told myself in an effort to rationalize my failure, the Safford Police Department had done no better.

I stopped at a traffic light and muttered ruefully. "Too bad there wasn't one of Weems' cameras in the classroom when Holderman was murdered."

I remembered the collection of Weems' photos on the walls of the chapel. And abruptly, a new piece for the puzzle appeared. That ethereal scrap of misjudged evidence. I couldn't believe it. Why hadn't I seen it before? That was it!

Shouting an ancestral expletive at the top of my lungs, I slammed the side of my fist against the steering wheel half-a-dozen times, each time screaming the expletive with growing enthusiasm.

Ecstatic, I looked around. Drivers on each side of me stared curiously, probably wondering when I was going to begin frothing at the mouth. I just gave them a stupid grin, and as soon as the light changed, sped away. I knew who had murdered George Holderman. And how. And why. It was as plain as the nose on my face, but I had been too blind to see it. Now all I had to do was prove it.

And I had a hunch how I could do that. It all depended on the answer Jim Hawkins, the teacher who provided the airtight alibi for Perry Jacobs, gave me.

At my office, I dialed his number. I asked him one simple question. He gave me the simple answer I wanted, the same one he'd given me before, but that I was too dumb to pick up on it. I thanked him, then dialed Harper Weems' number.

When Arthur Weems answered, I quickly explained what I had in mind and laid out my idea for a special reading of the will at the memorial service. That would give us time to notify everyone I had interviewed. "Tomorrow night, with your help, I'll show you who murdered your brother."

He agreed. I provided him a list of the suspects. Via his attorney, Weems contacted all, explaining that his brother had remembered that individual in his will and requested his presence when it was read at the memorial service.

I began making plans.

For once, Sergeant Chief Pachuca didn't laugh in my face. When I laid out my evidence, he stopped chomping on his ubiquitous cigar. "Ummm." He studied the plan. "What happens if they don't bite?"

"I thought of that. I've got license numbers of kids who made buys in the parking lot. I'm seeing them today. One of them will rat." I hesitated. "Don't sweat it, Chief. It'll work."

Chief Billy Vanbiber of the Safford Police Department agreed to be present also.

I spent the afternoon lining up the incriminating evidence. At 3:15, I called the sheriff's department. Vanderweg had been arrested and presently was residing in Travis County jail awaiting extradition.

Without replacing the receiver, I placed a call to Eddie Dyson. I kept my fingers crossed, hoping he had managed to shift most of Janice's last investment.

Eddie was effusive. "Tony. Tony. How you doing, my man? You're a good dude to do business with, you know? I always like doing business with you."

I frowned. He was almost delighted. That wasn't like Eddie. Or was he being sarcastic? Tentatively, I asked, "What happened, Eddie?"

"You made my week, Tony. The deal's done. One problem, I could only debit your account fifteen thousand. You owe me another eight. A total of twenty-three thousand."

My jaw dropped open. "Twenty-three thousand?" What in the dickens was going on? "Hey, Eddie. Ten percent. That's all you were supposed to charge."

"And that's what I did, Tony. The guy had two hundred and

thirty-one thousand in his account. I transferred it like you said. All except one G."

My brain raced. Two hundred and thirty thousand. Jeez.

Slowly, Eddie's voice cut through the roaring in my ears. "Tony, you okay? Hey, Tony."

"Huh? Oh, yeah. Yeah, I'm okay." I hesitated. "Eddie, are you sure?"

"Hey, I never make mistakes, Tony. That's part of the service."

Laughing weakly, I said, "Well, you gave me some good service this time. Thanks. I'll get the other eight to you, don't worry."

"I ain't worrying, Tony."

I sat staring at the receiver. It was almost four. The bank was closed. As soon as the bank opened in the morning, I'd draw out three cashier's checks, one for $15,000, one for $23,000, and the third for $85,000.

What about the other $107,000.00? What poor, trusting suckers did it belong to?

I've never been one who believed if you focused on a problem just before sleep, your dreams would solve it. However, that's the only explanation I can give for the dream I had that night. I awakened, laughing at just what I was going to do with the additional $107,000. Still chuckling at the idea, I turned over and went back to sleep.

Next morning, I opened the *Austin Daily News* and my eyes bulged out. On the front page was a shot of a frowning Nelson Vanderweg, and a headline story of a con man wanted throughout the country.

I shook my head as I read the story. The louse was worse than I thought, and I felt a sense of grim satisfaction that I had been responsible for the scuzzbag being nailed.

Using my fake identification, I stopped by the bank and withdrew the entire account, cut into four cashier's checks. The first,

$15,000, was for Alice Baglino in Arizona; the next, $23,000, I deposited in my own account to cover Eddie Dyson's commission; the third, $85,000, I put in my wallet to deliver to Janice Coffman-Morrison; the fourth and remaining $107,000, I mailed to the Austin PD with a letter explaining the origin of the funds. I also pointed out that I had placed a thirty-day advertisement in the *Austin Daily News* for investors whom Vanderweg had exploited to file claims for the return of their investments.

And then I promptly shredded Robert Rodison's identification.

Janice called me at the office, boohooing over Vanderweg's arrest. "Do you think it's really true, Tony?"

Her voice was so weak and pitiful, I did the gentlemanly thing. I lied. "Who knows?" I hesitated, not wanting to hurt her any more than she was hurting.

She persisted. "Do you . . . do you think you could find out for me, Tony? I mean, is it the truth or just the media?"

"Yeah. If you want. I can probably find out." I guess I should have felt guilty for lying, but I didn't.

"Would you, Tony. Would you, please?" She paused, then in a timorous voice, said, "I know I treated you badly, Tony. But, well, I . . ."

"Hey, forget it, Janice. I'm happy to help. Why don't I come over later, about one o'clock or so? I should know something by then."

The sheriff's department verified the truth of the news story. "Yeah," growled one of the deputies. "That mug has probably bilked lovelorn old spinsters out of millions. From what we heard, half-a-dozen other states are contacting Arizona for the guy." He laughed. "I hope he put away some of that loot. He's going to need one good lawyer."

I chuckled to myself. Eddie Dyson had left Vanderweg only $1,000. That's about all the lawyer he deserved.

Janice met me at the door, her eyes red from crying. To look at her, you wouldn't guess she was heir to a forty- or fifty-million-dollar estate. She looked as rundown and ragged as the harried mother of two-year-old triplets with the backdoor trots and front door heaves.

An honest remark would have been, "Janice, you look like death warmed over," but only if I wanted her to start crying all over again. Instead, I winked at her and lied. "You look great."

She blushed and rushed into my arms. "You're sweet, Tony, even if you are lying."

"I know." I hugged her and laughed.

"Come on in," she said, taking my hand and leading me into the living room. "Want a drink?"

"Yeah. You think you remember it?" I teased her.

She blushed. "Of course. It isn't hard. Straight bourbon, right?"

"You remembered, but why don't you just make it water."

We made small talk for a few minutes, each painfully aware we were tiptoeing around Nelson Vanderweg. Finally, she broached the subject. "What did you find out?"

I learned the hard way if I had to eat crow, it was better warm. Get it over with, straight, honest, blunt. I looked her straight in the eyes. "It isn't good. He was pulling a con. Half-a-dozen states have warrants out on him. Seems like he's taken over a million dollars from . . . from . . ."

Janice finished the sentence for me. "From stupid, foolish women like me." Tears welled in her eyes again. She dropped her chin to her chest.

I laid my hand on her arm. "You're not stupid or foolish. You believed him. Guys like that can stare you in the eyes and tell you anything. You're a sweet, trusting woman, and Nelson Vanderweg will never have any idea what he threw away in you."

She looked up at me, her eyes bright with gratitude. She leaned forward and kissed me. "Thank you, Tony."

Setting my water on the coffee table, I pulled out my wallet and unfolded the cashier's check. "This is for you."

"What is it?" She frowned and read the check. With a gasp, she looked up in disbelief. "But, this is the money I gave . . . how did you . . . I mean, where did this—"

"Don't ask. You didn't get it from me. No one knows you ever gave him anything. Just deposit it, and start putting all this behind you. In fact, maybe we can go out tomorrow night. That would be the first step."

Janice brushed her hair back from her eyes. "We could start tonight."

Talk about poor timing. "Sounds great, but I've got business to take care of tonight." I paused and grinned crookedly. "You want to give me a hand?"

She shook her head. "I told you before. I quit the PI business. You can have it."

I drained my water and rose to my feet. "I'll call you in the morning."

Chapter Thirty-six

The Crystal Creek Complex sprawled over and around the rugged hills near Lake Travis. Live oaks dotted the two-acre plots, each separated from adjoining plots by stone fences covered with lush vegetation. The swimming pools had been blasted out of the limestone bluffs and ledges, giving the impression of water standing in natural fissures along the hillsides. The overall image projected by the complex was of sylvan charm and elegant grace and obscene wealth. It was the kind of community that if you had to ask the price, it was too expensive for you.

I arrived early, anxious to set the stage.

The foyer of the mansion was the size of my entire apartment. To the left was the dining room; to the right, the living room where the service was to be held. You could fit three of my apartments in the living room.

Pictures of Harp and his brother filled the walls in chronological order, beginning from their infancy. At one end of the room was a small table, holding a cross with burning candles on either side. In front of the cross was a photo with Harp surrounded by several students.

Before everyone arrived at eight o'clock, Chief Pachuca took me aside. "What if the your killer doesn't show up?"

I arched an eyebrow and glanced at Billy Vanbiber. I looked back at Chief Pachuca and blew silently though my lips. "My killer is too smart not to show up."

He eyed me shrewdly. "Yeah. You're probably right this time, Boudreaux. One of the few times in your Cajun life, but you're probably right."

I grinned at his gentle sarcasm. "Thanks, Chief. Coming from you, I take it as a compliment."

He grunted and took his place in the kitchen. Vanbiber waited in the dining room.

For the first fifteen minutes, we all mixed and mingled, sipping punch and nibbling on catered bite-sized sandwiches. I made it a point to speak to everyone I had interviewed. Without exception, each was curious about my presence. I passed it off with the explanation that "I taught English once. Harp and I hit it off. I just wanted to pay my respects." The first and last lines were true.

Kim Nally and Frances Holderman chatted like long-lost sisters, a curious commentary on modern values. Perry Jacobs, Jim Hawkins, Henry Bishop, and Lionel Portis sat in a cluster in the middle of the room, probably discussing those brilliant concepts teachers debate such as lengthening or shortening the passing period between classes, or the importance of using pink hall passes instead of yellow hall passes.

Dorothy Saussy, Linda May, and Iona Flores formed another small group. Fred Seebell, the born-again Christian, and his wife stood apart from the others. A handful of students including Tim Briggs and Marvin Handwell stood around the table on which Harp's picture sat.

The stage was set.

Arthur Weems took his place beside the cross and tapped his ring against his glass. He ran his fingers through his inch-long hair. "Thank you all for coming." He gestured to the picture of Harper Weems on the table, his blond hair hanging down to his shoulders.

Clearing his throat, he continued. "Harp would be very proud of this display of friendship. Now, if everyone will find a seat, we'll get down to business."

He paused. Once everyone had found a seat, he cleared his throat. "Before we begin the service, Mr. Boudreaux has a few words to say."

I took a deep breath. Showtime.

He added, "While he has the floor, I need to check some items in the kitchen. Bring out a few more snacks." He hurried though the door as I stepped up beside the table.

From the kitchen came the muffled rattling of pots, a refrigerator door being opened and closed, cabinet drawers being opened, the general hubbub of food preparation.

I took a deep breath, trying to still the flutter in my stomach. I hoped my voice didn't start quivering. "As you all know, I investigated the murder of George Holderman." I paused, running my gaze around the room.

Perry Jacobs leaned forward in his chair, his eyes narrowing. Frances Holderman arched an eyebrow. Kim Nally looked bored. The students looked at each other and shrugged.

The rattling of pots and pans echoed from the kitchen.

"For several days, I was looking in the wrong place. I was puzzled because no one here fit the profile of the killer. Those with the motive did not have the opportunity. I was at a dead end until I saw Harper Weems' collection of photographs on the walls of the chapel. And even then, I didn't connect with the idea. That came later. Then I realized there was only one person who not only fit the profile, but also had the opportunity and motive. It just took me awhile to figure out the motive."

Several heads turned to look around the room.

Jacobs spoke up. "Who are you accusing, Boudreaux? If it's me, I'll sue your tail off."

I shook my head. "Relax, Jacobs. All of you can relax. In fact, everyone can relax." I deliberately focused on each individual, then added, "Everyone except two."

"Now what are you talking about?" Jacobs glared at me.

"There are two here who know what I mean." I turned to the cluster of students. "Isn't that right, Marvin, Tim?"

Marvin lurched forward on the couch. Tim remained motionless, but his eyes narrowed. He hissed between clenched teeth, "You're crazy. We were nowhere around Mr. Holderman. We were at the other end of the wing at the sign-in desk."

I grinned. "That was a slick trick, Tim. No wonder you're in the National Honor Society. I got to admit it. You're bright. Real bright. But you made a mistake." I nodded to Jim Hawkins. "When Hawkins signed in, there was only one of you at the desk. I didn't catch it at first, but I remembered he told me that he signed in with the boy in the hall." I turned to Hawkins. "Isn't that right?"

Hawkins nodded, his eyes blazing at the two boys. "Marvin was the only one there. Tim wasn't around."

"Hey, that's right," exclaimed Jacobs. "When Holderman and me signed it, Marvin was the only one there."

I continued. "The reason Tim wasn't around was because he was waiting in Jacobs' room for Holderman. In the closet." I fixed my eyes on Briggs. "I don't know exactly what the problem was, but I'm guessing Holderman had threatened to stop bankrolling you and Marvin in your drug business."

The muscular young man jumped to his feet, his fists clutched at his sides. "You're wiped out, dude. No way." He glanced around the room nervously.

"No. You're tall enough. You have the strength, and you're left-handed. Weems' photo of you throwing the football and holding your right arm out for balance is what made me realize you were the one." I shook my head. "I should have guessed when I saw the watch on your right wrist. Most of us wear our watches on our least dominant limb. I do. And you also do, Tim."

With fear in his eyes, Handwell looked up at Briggs anxiously.

Briggs rolled his massive shoulders. "I had no reason."

"Oh? Drugs isn't reason enough? I think it is. Remember the picture I took of you and Weems out at Lupe's? Where I made my mistake was in thinking he was offering you the bindle. That wasn't it at all, was it? He was trying to take the drugs from you, not sell them. Holderman bankrolled you. I don't know what happened between you and Holderman, but it had been going on a long time, all the way back to February 2001. You met Holderman monthly at Lupes'. And I'm sure it wasn't for tacos. Maybe you held out on him. Maybe he decided to dump you. I don't know, but you were the only one who could have killed him."

Handwell jumped to his feet. "No. We told you. Tim told you. Weems was dealing when we got to Safford."

No one spoke for a moment, and then, without warning, a shrill squeaking sliced through the silence. Everyone jerked around to stare toward the foyer.

The squeaking grew louder. The wheels thudded over the tile joints. In the kitchen, the rattling of pots and pans continued.

Abruptly, Harper Weems rolled into the living room. He shook his head. His long blond hair lay over his shoulders.

Everyone froze, stunned by the sudden apparition. Before anyone could speak, he glared at Briggs and Handwell. "It's payback time, boys. Next time you try to murder someone, make sure you do the job right."

With mouths gaping, everyone turned to the two high school seniors. Handwell blubbered, "I didn't want to, Mr. Weems. Honest. It was Tim." He ran forward and threw himself on the floor in front of the wheelchair. "I didn't want to. Please. I'm sorry. I'm sorry. I'm sorry."

"Shut up, Marvin." Tim's enraged voice echoed through the condo. "You dumb jerk. It's a trick. That's his twin brother."

"It might be a trick, Tim, but it worked," I said, starting toward him.

Arthur Weems rose from the wheelchair, anger and rage contorting his face. "You no good . . ."

Desperate, Tim spun toward the kitchen just as Chief Pachuca's bulky frame filled the door. The young man turned on me, his eyes dark with hate, his face twisted with rage. "You . . . you . . ."

"Give it up, Tim. You got no place to run."

Marvin continued blubbering on the floor while all the others sat in stunned disbelief.

With the roar of an enraged bull, the young killer turned and leaped through the leaded front window, shattering the glass and ripping out the metal mullions.

"Get him," yelled Pachuca, vaulting out the window into the darkness.

I was right behind the chief. "Where'd he go?"

"Around back. You go around the other side of the condo."

Vanbiber joined me in the chase. I didn't argue. Briggs was a husky young man in the prime of his life. I wasn't anxious to tackle him without another body or a ball bat. Preferably both.

Night had settled over the complex. Occasional shafts of light from streetlamps penetrated the canopy of leaves covering the grounds. The trees themselves were almost impossible to see until you were on top of them. Off to my right, I could hear Chief Pachuca huffing and groaning.

Ahead, a shadow cut across my course. I angled to my left. "This way!" I yelled, keeping the shadowy figure of Briggs in sight.

Behind me, I heard a thud and a groan. I didn't have time to look around. Ahead, Briggs hit the fence. I heard him scramble over. Seconds later, I followed, throwing myself over the fence and tumbling to the ground.

I rolled to my feet and peered into the darkness. I heard footsteps ahead of me. Far to my right was a commotion. "Over here, Chief!" I shouted, sprinting across the grassy yard after Briggs.

Suddenly, the high school senior screamed, and then I heard a splash. Seconds later, the ground went out from under my feet. Arms and legs windmilling, I flew through the air. A stray shaft of light from the streetlamps revealed a swimming pool beneath me.

I hit the water and slammed into Briggs, who instantly started punching at me with one hand and flailing water with the other. I swung back, and immediately sank.

I sputtered to the surface and swung at him, or where I thought he was, but the water slowed the blows. It's hard to deliver damaging punches while treading water. For that I was grateful. Briggs was tough and young and hard as a rock. His muscles had muscles, and mine, well, all I could say was I had what laughingly passed for muscles. If he could have planted his feet for leverage, I'd probably end up with my jaws wired together for three months.

We grappled. His fingers clawed at my face. A finger the size of a Louisiana sausage jammed into my mouth. I did what came naturally. I bit the heck out of it.

He screamed and jerked it loose, loosening also a couple of my incisors. He cursed and grunted and swung again. His bony knuckles bounced off my temple.

Karate-style, I jabbed my extended fingers at his face. They hit something soft, and he screamed. He lunged at me, slamming his plate-sized hands down on my shoulders and driving me underwater. He dug his fingers into my flesh, holding me down.

I twisted and struggled, wondering just where in the blazes Chief Pachuca and Vanbiber were. I was fast running out of breath. My ears roared. Red flashes exploded in my skull. I had to do something and fast, so I did what any red-blooded American male would do.

I hit him in the crotch.

And then I was free.

I slipped between his legs and came up behind him, throwing my arms around his throat and my legs around his waist. I squeezed as hard as I could. It was like trying to choke a tree trunk. "Now, you bag of sleaze, it's your turn." I grunted through clenched teeth.

Somewhere on the neck was a pressure point that should knock him out, but where? Choking and sputtering, I swore if I made it out of this mess that the first thing I would learn would be the exact location of that pressure point.

Cursing, he twisted and turned and rolled, trying to reach the shallow end of the pool. We were underwater more than above, but I clung like a tick on a dog's rear, clenching my teeth and squeezing for all I was worth. I felt his feet touch bottom.

Suddenly, he lunged backward, slamming me into the side of the pool. The back of my head cracked against the pool apron, bounced forward and slammed into the back of his head. He staggered forward, then threw himself backwards again.

Stars exploded in my head, but I held tight and squeezed harder. "Drop, blast you, drop."

Like an eight ball caroming off the pad, my head bounced off the pool apron again and slammed into the back of his head. A warm liquid ran down into my eyes. I struggled against the wave of dizziness threatening me. I didn't think I could stand one more blow to the back of my head.

Abruptly, Briggs went limp. We both sank under the water. I came up sputtering, but the shadows of the pool hid the high school senior from my sight. There was no splashing, which meant he was probably drowning. Good riddance, but I relented. I couldn't let him drown.

Easing forward, I felt with my feet. Off to my left, I found him. Gasping for breath, I dragged him to the shallow end of the pool and draped his torso across the pool deck, leaving his legs dangling in the water. I climbed out of the pool and stood over the dark shadow at my feet, ready to kick out his teeth if he tried anything.

Across the yard, I heard someone climbing the fence. "Boudreaux. You out there?"

It was Chief Pachuca. "Over here."

Feet pounded toward me. "Chief! Hey! Watch our for the swimming . . ."

A loud splash at the other end of the pool cut off my warning.

A water-soaked cop and a water-soaked PI with an equally water-soaked killer stood dripping water in the foyer of Weems' condo. I held a handkerchief to my forehead, which had split open when I hit the back of Tim's head.

Vanbiber sat on the couch, his head thrown back, a golfball-sized bloody knot on his forehead. He had straddled a tree in the dark.

Head down and sobbing, Handwell stood handcuffed between two Safford police officers. He had admitted everything.

Pachuca pushed Briggs toward them. "Here's the other one. You know what to do with them."

After the killers were taken away, Chief Pachuca grinned at me crookedly. "Well, Boudreaux, you got lucky."

Holding a paper napkin to my bleeding forehead, I let my shoulders sag. "Yeah, I guess I did." I looked around. "What I'd like right now is a stiff drink." I guess that moment was when I said goodbye to AA.

"Right this way," said Arthur Weems, leading the way to the wet bar in one corner of the living room, still wearing the blond wig.

I hesitated. "We'll drip on your carpet."

He gestured us in. "Who cares? Come on in. I'll get you another napkin for that head."

Perry Jacobs stepped forward. "How did you know it was them?"

I chuckled. "I didn't click on it at first. Then I remembered Briggs saying that Weems had tried to deal him some drugs four years ago. That's what Marvin was talking about tonight."

Jacobs frowned. "So?"

"Impossible. That's when Weems was convalescing from the accident in his van. He was staying with Arthur in Denver."

Kim Nally agreed. "I remember that. Harp wasn't teaching four years ago."

"But, why did they kill my brother?" Arthur Weems asked, tossing the wig on the snack bar.

"Just a guess, but I think your brother had an idea something was going on between the boys and Holderman. One night at Lupes' Tacos, I saw Harper try to take some drugs from Tim. I think he wanted to help the boys, get them to stop before it was too late. Maybe he threatened to go to the cops."

Frances Holderman cleared her throat. "You think he might have figured out they killed my husband?"

I finished off my bourbon. "Chances are, he did. From my days in the classroom, I remember being very aware of the undercurrents among students. Kids can't keep secrets. Sooner or later, they've got to tell someone, if only to brag."

Arthur Weems studied the glass of bourbon in his hand. "So, what you're telling me is that Harper got himself killed because he was trying to help some high school kids." He looked at me, and I could see a flash of bitterness in his eyes.

I looked around the room. Everyone was looking at me. "Arthur, a teacher is a very special person. He has a knack, an affinity for kids. If you don't have that gift, teaching is a miserable job. If you do, you make a big contribution to the world. You might not think it then, but it's true, nevertheless. So, to answer your question, yes. Harper got himself killed because he was trying to help kids."

I grinned at Chief Pachuca who had knocked down three fingers of scotch. "I promise one thing. By the time Marvin stops crying, you'll know everything there is to know."

Chief Pachuca nodded slowly and held up his glass in a toast to my prediction.

Chapter Thirty-seven

They say that death and luck run in threes.

What happened next made me a believer in that maxim.

I felt pretty smug during the drive to my apartment that night. This had been a big day. Janice had her $85,000 back in the bank; Vanderweg was where he deserved to be; two murders were solved; Frances Holderman was happy; Marty Blevins, my boss, would be ecstatic; I would be $5,000 ahead; and the Universal Life Insurance Company would close their eyes and weep.

My apartment was dark when I pulled up out front. My head had stopped bleeding, and I was anxious for a hot shower and a warm bed, but first, I nuked some milk for Cat, only to discover the little feline had disappeared. I searched the apartment and the shrubbery outside the door.

He was gone. He must have darted out when I opened the door. I shrugged. Just as well, I told myself. I didn't need another pet anyway, but I was going to miss the little guy.

Just as I started back into my apartment, a police cruiser pulled up at the curb and the uniform called out. "Tony Boudreaux?"

Puzzled, I replied, "Yeah."

"A cadaver came into the morgue with your name and address in his pocket. We need you to identify the body if you can."

My ears roared. All I could do was gape at the officer.

The dash lights of the cruiser illuminated the concern on his face. "Mr. Boudreaux, are you all right?"

I managed to choke out a single question. "A black man?"

"Yeah."

"Young?"

He nodded.

Nausea swept over me, knotting my stomach. I cursed myself all the way to the morgue.

It was Stewart. Gangland execution. Hands behind back, bullet in back of head.

Austin PD dropped me off at my place just after 2 A.M.

With my insides ripped out, I watched until the black and white disappeared around the corner. I stared up at the cold, impersonal stars and thought of Harper Weems who died trying to help kids, and I thought of myself. "At least," I muttered to the twinkling stars, "we both tried to help, Harp. We might not have made it, but we tried, and nobody can take that from us."

But, as I stood on the porch, staring up into the starry heavens, I wondered if there had been something else I could have done, should have done. Or was it, according to the French writer, Anatole France, simply chance, that pseudonym God uses when He doesn't want to sign His name?

I closed my eyes and prayed that when I opened them, the sun would be brightly shining.

It wasn't.

Reluctantly, I opened the door and went inside. Now, I faced making the hardest telephone call of my life.